The secret

With one abrupt movement, the man thrust his bundle through the open door. "Take the baby," he said baldly. "The child is not safe in anyone else's hands."

With a soft exclamation of surprise, the woman placed her candle on a nearby table and accepted the infant into her arms. "But whose child is this?" she murmured, looking down into the small sleeping face and beginning to rock slowly back and forth on the balls of her feet.

"I will whisper the name into your ear," the man said, coming near enough to do just that. "It is a secret."

She nodded, and he brought his mouth so close to her face he might have been kissing her on the cheek. She listened, nodded again, and looked him directly in the eyes as he straightened up and drew back.

"I will tell my sister," she said.

"And no one else," he said.

"And no one else," she repeated.

~ ꝏ ~

FIREBIRD
WHERE FANTASY TAKES FLIGHT™

Books by Sharon Shinn

The Safe-Keeper's Secret

SHARON SHINN

FIREBIRD

AN IMPRINT OF PENGUIN GROUP (USA) INC.

FIREBIRD

Published by the Penguin Group

Penguin Group (USA) Inc., 345 Hudson Street, New York, New York 10014, U.S.A.

Penguin Group (Canada), 90 Eglinton Avenue East, Suite 700, Toronto,
Ontario, Canada M4P 2Y3
(a division of Pearson Penguin Canada Inc.)

Penguin Books Ltd, 80 Strand, London WC2R 0RL, England

Penguin Ireland, 25 St Stephen's Green, Dublin 2, Ireland
(a division of Penguin Books Ltd)

Penguin Group (Australia), 250 Camberwell Road, Camberwell,
Victoria 3124, Australia (a division of Pearson Australia Group Pty Ltd)

Penguin Books India Pvt Ltd, 11 Community Centre, Panchsheel Park,
New Delhi - 110 017, India

Penguin Group (NZ), Cnr Airborne and Rosedale Roads, Albany, Auckland 1310,
New Zealand (a division of Pearson New Zealand Ltd)

Penguin Books (South Africa) (Pty) Ltd, 24 Sturdee Avenue,
Rosebank, Johannesburg 2196, South Africa

Registered Offices: Penguin Books Ltd, 80 Strand, London WC2R 0RL, England

First published in the United States of America by Viking,
a division of Penguin Young Readers Group, 2004
Published by Firebird, an imprint of Penguin Group (USA) Inc., 2005

1 3 5 7 9 10 8 6 4 2

THE LIBRARY OF CONGRESS HAS CATALOGED THE VIKING EDITION AS FOLLOWS:
Shinn, Sharon.
The Safe-Keeper's secret / by Sharon Shinn.
p. cm.
Summary: Fiona is Safe-Keeper in the small village of Tambleham,
where neighbors and strangers alike come one by one, in secret,
to tell her things they dare not share with anyone else.
ISBN 0-670-05910-2 (hardcover)
[1. Secrets—Fiction. 2. Villages—Fiction.] I. Title.
PZ7.S5572Saf 2004 [Fic]—dc22 2003023538

ISBN 0-14-240357-1

Printed in the United States of America

∾ FOR AARON ∿

Because reading the last few chapters aloud to you
is one of my most special memories.

A truth comes out when it must;

A dream comes true when it will.

Though the world turn to ash and dust,

A secret's a secret still.

The Safe-Keeper's Secret

Prologue

he solitary horse and rider clattered through the sleeping town, iron-shod hooves striking sharply against the half-buried cobblestones of the market square. Twenty yards outside the village green, the road turned to dirt again, and the animal's feet made only a muted thud against the dry soil. It was still an urgent sound, for the horse was moving fast—as fast as it could after a long night of hard running.

The rider only slowed as he passed the last houses on the road leading out of town. He bent to peer at each lawn and roofline, clearly looking for a mark or signal. Not till he came to the small gray-brick cottage on the very edge of Tambleham did he pull the horse to a complete halt.

A spray of roses by the gate, dark and colorless in the moonlight. A low hedge of no particular shape or beauty. And a kirrenberry tree planted by the front door.

A Safe-Keeper's house.

Moving awkwardly because of a bundle clutched tightly to his chest, the rider dismounted and led his horse through

1

the gate. There he let the exhausted animal stand untethered while he hurried up the flagged walkway and knocked on the front door. When there was no immediate answer, he pounded even louder.

A moment later, a young woman opened the door, holding a candlestick that illuminated her face. Despite the lateness of the hour, she looked wide awake and not at all alarmed at the appearance of this midnight visitor. Her dark hair was pinned to the back of her head, and her yellow gown appeared to be spattered with a variety of stains.

"Yes?" she asked.

Her visitor was not nearly so calm. "You are the Safe-Keeper of this village?" he demanded in a low voice.

She shook her head. "No. I—"

He fell back a step, clutching his bundle even more tightly to him. "No! But you—but the kirrenberry tree—"

"My sister is Safe-Keeper here. I am Safe-Keeper in Lowford, thirty miles over that hill."

He stepped forward again, instantly reassured. Any Safe-Keeper was to be trusted, no matter where he or she could be found. "Where is your sister? I must speak with her."

She gave him the tiniest of smiles. "My sister cannot come to the door now. She is in labor and will soon be delivered of a child."

Now he backed off again, turning away as if to shield the package in his arms from anyone else's sight. "Is she—is there a midwife in the house? Another woman from the town to aid you?"

The young woman shook her head. "No. Just my sister

2

and me. I have delivered plenty of babies in Lowford. I know what to do."

He stood there a moment longer, undecided, but it was clear from the set of his shoulders that he was weary almost beyond imagining. "I can go no farther," he said at last, seeming to speak to himself more than the woman at the door. "I have ridden as long and as hard as I can. I must leave my secret with you."

Just then there was a wail from inside the house, the long, indignant moan of a woman who was not enjoying her circumstances. "Quickly, then," the woman said. "I must go to her."

With one abrupt movement, the man thrust his bundle through the open door. "Take the baby," he said baldly. "The child is not safe in anyone else's hands."

With a soft exclamation of surprise, the woman placed her candle on a nearby table and accepted the infant into her arms. "But whose child is this?" she murmured, looking down into the small sleeping face and beginning to rock slowly back and forth on the balls of her feet.

"I will whisper the name into your ear," the man said, coming near enough to do just that. "It is a secret."

She nodded, and he brought his mouth so close to her face he might have been kissing her on the cheek. She listened, nodded again, and looked him directly in the eyes as he straightened up and drew back.

"I will tell my sister," she said.

"And no one else," he said.

"And no one else," she repeated.

"Will she keep the baby? Will you?"

"Or we will find a home that is safe," she said gently. "Your secret is ours to keep now."

"Then I must go back," he said.

There was another cry from the back of the house, this one a little sharper. But the young woman lingered at the doorway, her worried gaze on her visitor. "What will become of you, when you return to the city and this one is missing?" she asked.

He shook his head. "I know what I must do next. Have no fear for me."

A pitiful cry came from the back room. "Angeline! Where have you gone?"

"Who are you?" she asked. "I will tell no one. Just so I know."

For the first time since she had opened the door to him, he smiled, a rather grim expression. "I am the Safe-Keeper to the king," he said.

"*Angeline!*"

"Safe passage home," she said.

"My deepest thanks," he replied. Finally relieved of his burden, he lost some of his desperation and acquired a certain courtly air. He gave her a deep, flourishing bow, and kissed his fingers to her as he swept upright.

"When should the secret be told?" she asked.

"You will know," he said. "But it will not be soon."

"*Angeline! I need you!*"

"Good-bye, then," she said.

"Good-bye," he said. Turning with a swirl of his cloak,

4

he headed back to his horse. By the time he had led the tired animal through the gate and climbed back into the saddle, the door to the cottage was already closed. There was no sign of either woman or baby.

In the morning, Elminstra was the first one to come knocking on the Safe-Keeper's door. She had a loaf of fresh-baked bread in one hand and a bucket of milk in the other, for she was sure Angeline had had no time to be thinking of food, and Damiana was in no condition.

"Hello?" she called, pushing the door open when no one responded to her knock. She was the nearest neighbor, living a mere quarter mile down the road, and she and Damiana quite freely walked into each other's houses. "Angeline? Damiana? Has the baby come?"

Just as Elminstra stepped into the big main room, Angeline came in from the kitchen, cradling a child in each arm. "In fact, two babies have come," Angeline said, smiling.

With a little shriek, Elminstra dropped both her loaf and her bucket to the floor. "Twins! I would swear she was not big enough to be carrying two—are they early? Are they healthy? Let me see them, the precious little ones—"

"Not twins," Angeline said, handing one of the children to the neighbor. Elminstra was a grandmother herself, though she looked more of an age to be a mother, and she had handled more babies in her time than Angeline and her sister put together. "This little girl was born around three in the morning. But this young man"—and she glanced down into the face of the baby she had kept in her arms—"he

5

arrived a few hours earlier when a strange rider brought him to our door."

Elminstra, who had begun cooing into the blankets she held, looked up sharply at this statement. "So I didn't dream it!" she exclaimed. "I thought I heard a horse go by late last night, very fast. It was someone coming here?"

Angeline nodded. "And leaving a package behind."

The baby girl made a sound halfway between a whimper and a cough, and Elminstra began to jiggle her absently. "But—who was he? And whose child did he bring to you?"

Angeline merely smiled, and Elminstra nodded. Being neighbor to a Safe-Keeper for so long had taught her not to expect answers to all her questions. Not that many of those answers would surprise her. She was a healer and herbalist—some called her a witch—and people often came to her for medicines and remedies that some other woman might find shocking.

"Will she keep this baby, then? Or will you?" Elminstra asked.

"I was willing to take him back to Lowford, but Damiana is determined to keep him," Angeline said. "She says it's easier for one person to raise two babies than for two people to raise one apiece, though I'm not so sure that's true. But she thinks these two will be company for each other as they grow older."

"Company for each other, and enemies with each other, and mischief-makers who incite each other to even greater mischief," Elminstra said with feeling. "She could be right! But on the other hand, it is not such an easy thing to raise a child all by yourself—and to raise two children"—

6

Elminstra shook her head. "I don't suppose," she added delicately, "this makes her any more interested in contacting her daughter's father and seeing if he would be willing to help her out?"

Angeline grinned. "No, nor has it made her any more interested in divulging the identity of her daughter's father."

Elminstra sighed and continued bouncing the baby in her arms. "There is some talk about Damiana already, you know, choosing to have a child all on her own and telling no one who the father is. Oh, everyone loves her, of course—"

"Everyone loves their Safe-Keeper," Angeline interrupted. "She knows too many secrets for them *not* to love her."

"But now with *two* children in the house—well, it will cause even more talk."

Angeline shrugged and patted the child's back. "Such things don't bother Damiana. I think she'll raise both children and she'll be happy and they'll be happy, and there won't be any more talk."

"Until the secret about the child's parentage comes out," Elminstra said.

Angeline laughed. "Which one?"

Elminstra was still in the Safe-Keeper's house when the next visitor came calling, and the next, and the next. To each of them, Angeline told the same story, of the boy delivered to the house at midnight and the girl delivered to the bed three hours later. Everyone was agog with curiosity—but, like Elminstra, they knew the futility of questioning a Safe-Keeper. Angeline would reveal no secrets now, and

Damiana would reveal no secrets later. In fact, Damiana appeared likely to stay in her bed sleeping the entire day through, waking up only enough to nurse both infants whenever they started to wail.

"You'll need milk," Elminstra said briskly. "She won't have enough for both of them. I'll bring you a bucket every morning."

"How long are you staying?" Lacey asked Angeline. She was seamstress in Tambleham and friendly with everybody. "I imagine they'll be wanting you back in Lowford very soon. I can come once a day to help with dinner."

Other women chimed in with similar offers, and Angeline accepted them all on behalf of her sister. Damiana was the kind who could manage entirely on her own; but Damiana also had the ability to accept aid with great grace and sweetness. It was one of the reasons everyone in Tambleham liked her so much. That and her ready smile and her sweet face and her gift for silence. She was just the sort of person you would want to have for your friend, no matter what you needed a friend for.

It was past lunchtime, and Elminstra had taken over the kitchen to prepare a meal for everyone, when running footsteps could be heard coming up the walk. All the women glanced at each other—there were eight of them by now, enjoying the chance to gossip and in no mood to go back to their own uninteresting chores when there were babies to be played with—and wondered aloud who might be approaching in such a hurry.

It was Dirk, the tavern-keeper's son, a promising and

8

very large young man of about eighteen. "Have you heard?" he demanded, bursting into the house with all the vigor of youth having an exciting story to tell. "They've found a dead man on the road, not ten miles south of town."

All the women cried out in worry and alarm. "Who is it?" "No one from Tambleham, I hope!" "What happened? Bandits?" "Oh, please tell me the poor man simply fell from his horse."

"What happened?" Angeline asked, raising her voice enough to be heard over all the other women. Dirk turned in her direction.

"A man. A stranger. He was dressed in fine clothes and wearing a black cloak lined with red silk," the boy said. "His horse was tied to the side of the road, and there were twenty gold pieces in one of his saddlebags. Jewels on his fingers, expensive leather shoes on his feet."

The women exchanged glances. "He was not killed for his possessions, then," Angeline said.

"But—a rich man like that—what was he doing alone on the road—here by Tambleham?" Elminstra said. "And who would have had reason to kill him if not to rob him?"

Dirk was shaking his head. "My father says that no one killed him," he said. "My father says he put poison in a cup and drank it down. There was a silver goblet lying on the ground not three feet from his hand, and my father said the smell of wine was tainted."

"But then—but who—" one of the neighbor women said.

But Elminstra was staring at Angeline, who was taking a sip from her own cup. "A rich man riding alone at night a few miles outside our village," the witch said slowly. "Could this have been the man who came to visit you last night, leaving a baby at your sister's door?"

"I suppose it could be," Angeline said.

"But why would he do such a thing?" Lacey demanded. "If he knew he had left the child in safe hands, why would he then take his own life?"

Angeline said nothing, but Elminstra was still puzzling it out. "Because he wanted no one to find out where he had taken the child," she guessed. "He wanted no one to question him so ruthlessly that he might accidentally reveal where the child had gone."

"But what child would be so special that a man would have to give his life to protect it?" Dirk demanded.

And then suddenly, everyone in the room fell silent as they all stared at Angeline.

"The man was on his way back to Wodenderry," said Dirk slowly. "The royal city."

"Do we have a king's bastard in our village?" Elminstra asked in a very faint voice.

Just then, one of the babies began a slow, mournful howling from the other room. Angeline smiled at them all, giving away no secrets. "Royal bastard or village bastard, someone is calling me," she said cheerfully. "Let me go see what my niece and nephew want."

And she disappeared into the room where her sister lay, tending to two infants. Dirk and the women were left staring at each other, their faces pale and their hearts scampering madly in their chests. What a tale to be told tonight over garden fences and barroom tables! What magic had visited their village last night—indeed, come to live with them, nestled into the corners and alleys of their town! A king's bastard! Who would have believed it? Everyone would know by nightfall. This was a Safe-Keeper's house, of course, but this was surely one secret that would not be kept.

~ ✏ ~

Part

Chapter One

Fiona had assigned names to all her dolls, and she was arranging them by how much she loved each of the people those dolls represented.

Her mother, of course, was first, followed closely by her brother, Reed. Her aunt Angeline was next, then Elminstra, then Lacey and Isadora. Of all the people she knew, Thomas was the very last, the person she liked least, and she not only put him at the end of the long line of dolls, she tossed him across the room so that his head landed under the bed.

Unfortunately, Thomas was visiting her mother's house this week, and she would have to be polite to him even though she didn't want to.

She had always liked Thomas just fine, until the last time he had come to visit. He was a Truth-Teller, a wanderer who went from village to village answering such questions as were posed to him and volunteering information that people might not have wanted to hear. Fiona was not the only one who disliked him because he had told her something that she would rather have believed was not true.

But Truth-Tellers could not lie. Falsehoods could not cross their lips. Anything they said had to be believed.

"Fiona's growing into a fine young girl, isn't she?" he'd said to her mother last time he was here. They'd all been sitting around the table, eating sweet apples and enjoying the late light of a midsummer evening. All except Reed, who'd been off playing with one of Elminstra's grandsons. "How old are you now? Eight?"

"I'll be ten this fall," she had replied.

"Ten! So old! A woman grown before you know it," he had said. He had a way of laughing when he talked, even when he told unpleasant facts, which was one of the reasons people did not like him. They thought he mocked them with unpalatable truths. He was gaunt and weathered from so much travel, and his dark hair and his curly beard were both a little unkempt. His brown eyes were set back in deep hollows, as though he looked out from a place of shadow on all the verities of the world.

"She's going to apprentice with Elminstra in a few years," her mother said in her quiet voice. "Learn about herbing. She's already better in the garden than I am."

"Not that that would take much," Thomas said with a snort.

Fiona was offended, but her mother grinned. "I do well enough with tomatoes and beets. But Fiona can make anything grow."

"Maybe she'll be the village witch, then, after Elminstra's time is done," Thomas said.

"No," Fiona said. "I'm going to do my mother's work. I'll be a Safe-Keeper."

16

Thomas had looked straight at her with those deep and knowing eyes. "No," he said, "you won't."

Fiona had cried out in quite a fit of anger, but he had merely shrugged and peeled another apple. "I will *so* be a Safe-Keeper if I want to be," Fiona had said again, glancing at her mother for support. But her mother had merely given her that quiet smile, hiding all her thoughts.

"You'll be what you choose to be," Damiana had said, refusing to get into an argument or contradict Thomas or even seem to worry about what he had said.

"I *hate* you," Fiona had declared, stomping from the room. And no one had chided her for that and neither had Damiana mentioned the whole incident later that night when she came to tuck the children into bed.

But Fiona *did* hate him, and she wished he was not here at her birthday party. She would just as soon not turn ten with Thomas the Truth-Teller sitting there, watching her with his considering eyes.

Reed came to find her in her room a few minutes after she had rearranged her dolls, putting Isadora before Lacey after all. They shared the small upstairs loft, its sloped ceiling so low that Reed would not long be able to stand upright under its beams. A sturdy wall divided her neat half from his untidy one.

"Fiona! Where are you? What are you doing? It's almost time to eat."

"I'm just playing," she called out.

He bounded through the door and landed with a bounce

on her bed. Almost instantly, he changed his mind, scrambled to his feet, and dropped to the floor beside her. He could never sit still, this brother of hers; he was always charging off in one direction or another.

"Well, aren't you done playing by now?" he asked, his voice carefully patient. He had learned a long time ago that it was very difficult to hurry Fiona. If she wanted to sit here till dawn of the next day, dressing and organizing her dolls, sit here she would, even if the whole town gathered downstairs for a feast in honor of her birthday.

"Almost. Who's here?" she asked.

"Elminstra and two of her daughters and three of her grandchildren, and Dirk and his wife—oh, and their baby!—and his dad, and Josh and Ned—"

"Is Angeline here?"

He jumped to his feet and began to circle the room, touching the curtain, the oak dresser, the nightstand, in turn. "Not yet. But she said she might be late. She said not to wait dinner for her."

"But I don't want to eat without Angeline!"

"Well, everybody else does! It smells really good and everyone is *hungry*."

"I don't want to have to sit by Thomas."

"Fine. I'll sit with Thomas. Greg and I will trip him if he tries to come over and talk to you."

Greg was Elminstra's grandson, three months older than Reed. "I didn't say I wanted you to do anything to him—"

"Just come downstairs and eat," Reed said impatiently, coming to a halt in the middle of her hierarchy of dolls.

"It's your birthday! We can't have the feast without you!"

She glanced up at him and smiled. For children who were not related by blood, they looked surprisingly alike. Both had fair skin and silky blond hair, Fiona's hair finer and whiter than Reed's, and both had slim, wiry builds that concealed their true strength. Reed was inexhaustible, able to run or play or even work tirelessly throughout the day. Fiona was not so active, but she knew she could endure almost anything. She had nearly cut a finger off one morning, slicing sweetroot at Elminstra's, and she hadn't even cried out when the knife went in. She had suffered every childhood disease without the smallest protest, and once, when she had fallen off a broad stone fence that she had been climbing, she had cracked her head open on a rock buried in the ground. She had not complained about that, either, not the littlest bit.

"It's your birthday, too," she said. "They can't have the feast without you either."

"Yes, but *I'm* going downstairs right this minute," he said. "Please come? Make it a special day?"

She put her hand out and he pulled her to her feet. Already he was an inch or two taller than she was; everyone predicted he would be a big, strapping boy, one of those fair, happy yeomen who could be found standing at the ale booth at every county fair.

"It *is* a special day," she said, and kissed him on the cheek. "Happy birthday."

She followed him downstairs to find everything ready for the feast and the thirty or so neighbors gathered there

19

quite ready to begin eating. A little cheer sounded when she and Reed appeared, and they were pushed to the front of the line that had formed around the table. "Birthday children are the first to eat!" someone cried. Fiona loaded up her plate and took it outside to where a grand mismatch of tables and chairs had been arrayed on the lawn, and she and Reed both settled in. Soon enough everyone was gathered around them, Damiana sitting next to Fiona, Greg beside Reed, Elminstra on the other side of Damiana, and all the other neighbors falling in as they chose. The food—potluck supplied by all the visiting friends—was delicious, and there was so much of it that nobody felt too greedy going back for seconds, or even thirds.

Thomas, who could usually be found right by Damiana's side any time he was in town, spent most of his time in conversation with Dirk and his father, a fact that Fiona viewed with darkling satisfaction. He must have realized that he had offended her on his last visit and was making amends by keeping out of her way now. That pleased her very much, but not so much as it would if he took back his words altogether.

"Mmm! This cherry pie is heavenly! Who could have made it?" Elminstra exclaimed.

"Ned's wife, I think. She said she had a new recipe," Damiana replied.

"Well, she came by to get cherries from me last week, but she didn't say she was going to make anything this good."

"I liked the baked chicken," Lacey put in. "What spices do you suppose she used? Mine never turns out quite like that."

"Dill and thyme," Elminstra and Fiona said in unison, because it was the sort of thing any herbalist would know, and Fiona was taking pride in her ability to recognize all sorts of plants by their smell and flavor.

Elminstra beamed at her. "That's my girl! I'll have to send you to my sister over in Merendon some day. She can grow a whole field of crops that won't take purchase here."

"Yes, please," Fiona said. "I'd like that."

Her mother reached over and tugged one of Fiona's blond braids. "Not for a while yet," she said. "You're so little and Merendon is so far away. I want you to stay with me a while longer yet."

"Oh, of course I will," Fiona said earnestly. "I'll stay as long as you need me."

This caused the other women to laugh, which caused Fiona to scowl. But she didn't have long to pout, because from the front of the house came the sound of a wagon creaking and a horse whickering.

"Is this the party?" came a woman's voice, somewhat faint as it carried around the house.

"Angeline!" Fiona shrieked. Reed was on his feet even before she was. They raced around the vegetable garden at the back of the house, ducked under the branches of the kirrenberry tree, and leaped over the gate without bothering to unlatch it. Angeline was just then climbing down from the wagon, and she flung her arms out to offer them an embrace.

"Look at you two! Reed, have you grown *again*? Fiona, your hair's so long! It's only been three months since

I've seen you—how can you have changed so much?"

They hugged her and danced around her and swore that they hadn't changed, not on the *inside*, and look, didn't she want to come in and see Reed's new slingshot, Fiona's new dolls?

"In a bit, yes, indeed, I want to see everything," Angeline said with a laugh. "But first I must get my bags from the cart and say good-bye to my friends—"

Damiana spoke up from behind them, having come around the house in a more leisurely fashion. "Well, hello there," she said in her warm voice. "I didn't realize Angeline was coming to town with the two of you. Are you staying for dinner? There's so much food!"

Till now, Fiona had paid no attention to the couple sitting in the front of the wagon, but at her mother's words, she looked up to see if she recognized them. The man and the woman looked pleasant enough, but Fiona was sure she'd never met them before. The woman was fair-haired and fragile-looking, wearing a fashionable blue dress over her brittle frame. Her companion was more hearty and robust, a well-dressed, wealthy-looking man with a kind expression. Fiona thought he was probably a merchant, since he certainly didn't appear to be a laborer. She thought his wife looked boring.

"We can't stay," the woman said in a faint voice, seeming to need all her energy to summon a smile. "I want to go to the inn and lie down."

"Victoria tires so easily," the man said, apology in his voice. "But I understand you're having quite a party here! A birthday celebration for these two young folks, is that right?"

"Yes, sir. We're ten, sir," said Reed. He had already moved to the front of the wagon and was inspecting the horses. "I like your team! Matched bays! May I pet them?"

"Very gently. The gelding on the left is a little edgy, but the mare on the right won't mind."

Fiona was still looking up at the new arrivals, thinking no one should be tired if all she'd done all day was sit in a wagon, when her aunt's voice came gently in her ear. "Fiona, you remember Robert and Victoria Bayliss, don't you?" she said. "They live near me in Lowford, and they came by to visit two summers ago when you were staying with me."

"She wasn't home that day," Reed volunteered, his hand busy against the arched neck of the mare. "Remember? She'd gone off to the dress shop with your friend. But I was home. I remember you."

"Well, and I remember you! You've grown half a foot since that day, though," Robert said genially.

"You're sure you won't come in just for a bit?" Damiana said. "I could brew some tea, Victoria. It will pick up your spirits a little. And there's wonderful pie."

"Thank you. It's not my spirits but my body that's frail," Victoria said, again making the effort to smile. "If I could rest for just a while—"

"I've got everything I need," Angeline said briskly. "Go on into town. Thank you so much for the ride!"

"We'll be back in a few days to pick you up," Robert said,

gathering the reins. "Young man, if you'll step aside, we'll be on our way. Happy birthday to the both of you!"

And with a wave, he set the horses in motion. Victoria could not be bothered to wave, but she did smile again and give them a little nod before the wagon pulled out of sight.

Reed went running back to the party, but the two women stood there a moment as if to gossip, and Fiona stayed beside them to listen.

"She's no better, then?" Damiana asked. Fiona supposed she was referring to the wan Victoria.

"I do think she is in pain much of the time," Angeline said. "I try not to hold it against her that she is such a poor and sickly thing. But Robert is so hale and energetic! It is a little sad to see him tied to her like that."

"Though I think he loves her," Damiana said.

"He is certainly good to her," Angeline replied.

"Who is she? Who are they? Why does she act like that?" Fiona interrupted.

The woman exchanged glances and private smiles. "They are friends of mine from Lowford," Angeline said, her hand coming to rest on Fiona's head. "Robert is my land-lord, and charges me almost no rent at all. Victoria has me sew all her clothes, because she says only I know how to set a stitch that doesn't scratch her. Indeed, their patronage has made it very easy for me to live in Lowford all alone and not worry very much about money."

"But why does she act that way?" Fiona asked. "All bent over and hurt-looking like that?"

"I suppose because she really does hurt," Angeline said.

"There was an accident when she was a young woman. She got swept out of her father's boat and washed downriver. She was missing for weeks, and everybody thought she was dead. But then she returned, bruised and broken, having fetched up some miles downriver in a town where she knew no one, too sick to speak. It was only when some kind people there nursed her back to health that she could tell them where she belonged."

"Robert was quite taken with grief in the weeks she was missing," her mother added.

"Why?" Fiona said. She didn't think Victoria seemed like the kind of person anyone would miss.

"Because she was engaged to marry him, and he thought he had lost her forever."

"I don't think I'd have wanted her to come back if she was going to come back like that," Fiona said.

"Fiona!" her mother and her aunt said at the same time. Her mother added, in the voice of gentle reprimand that was her harshest form of punishment, "That's an unkind thing to say. You, with all the advantages of youth and health, should be kindest of all to someone who is weak and in pain."

Fiona shrugged. "I'll try," she said, "if I ever see her again."

Angeline shook her head a little, as if to say, *What can you expect from a ten-year-old girl?* "Now," she said, more briskly. "Where's this food I've been hearing about? I'm very hungry—and unlike Victoria, I can certainly eat!"

After the meal, it was time for gifts. Between them, Fiona and Reed opened box after box of treasures, including dolls and soldiers and a variety of games. They were both well pleased with the assortment. Indeed, Greg and Reed and a few of the other boys immediately set up a round of ring-toss and began running back and forth across the lawn with as much energy as they had shown at the start of the very long day.

"Doesn't sit still too much, does he?" Thomas inquired, coming to sit by Angeline and Damiana and Fiona.

Damiana laughed. "I would say never," she said. "He's like a bright fire on the kitchen hearth. He burns without ceasing."

Thomas nodded at Fiona, though she kept her eyes on her new doll and pretended he had not joined them. "And this one?"

Damiana reached out a hand to stroke Fiona's hair. "This one is like a coal in the firepit. Cool to look at but blazing with heat within."

Fiona could feel that the Truth-Teller was still watching her. "Come with me to the front of the house," he said. "I have a present for you, but it needs explaining."

The two women looked over at Fiona, for they could tell, if he could not, that she had set her mind against Thomas and might not be eager to go. But she shrugged and laid her doll aside and stood up.

"All right," she said.

A few months ago, he would have taken her hand and led her around the house, but today he did not try. He just walked in silence beside her as they passed the garden and rounded the corner and came to rest under the still, spreading branches of the kirrenberry tree. Kirrenberry trees never grew very tall or very broad, but their flat, dark leaves were wide and dense, and if you stood beneath one on the sunniest day, you would stand in absolute shadow.

"Last time I was here," Thomas said, running his hand down the smooth bark of the thick trunk, "your mother allowed me to trim a couple of branches and take them with me for whittling. I made two whistles, one for your brother and one for you."

Fiona frowned a little. "I've never heard of anyone making a whistle from a kirrenberry tree," she said.

"No, and I'll show you why," he agreed. He pulled a small flute out of a pocket in his vest. The wood was light colored and prettily marked with darker swirls and flecks the size of a bird's eye. He had strung it on a black silk cord so she could wear it around her neck. "Here. Blow into it and make a melody if you can."

Fiona gave him a sharp glance, then took the whistle from his hand. Putting her mouth against the blowhole and her fingers on the openings of the pipe, she breathed in.

But no sound came out.

She tried again and again, each time blowing harder, but the whistle would issue no music. "I don't understand," she said at last. "Why doesn't it work? Is it broken?"

Thomas shook his head. He was still standing with his hand against the trunk of the tree, watching her with his shadowed eyes. "Because a kirrenberry tree won't make a sound," he said. "You can cut its branches to make two sticks that you hit together along with the beat in a reel—but they make no sound. Hit it with an ax and the tree yields up no ringing noise. Fell it in the forest, and you will not hear it toppling to the ground. A whistle makes no music. Birds who land in its branches forget their own songs."

Now she was frowning. "That makes no sense."

He nodded. "That's why the kirrenberry tree is planted in front of the house of every Safe-Keeper in every village from here to the Cormeon Sea. Because a kirrenberry tree signifies silence."

She lifted her head; now she understood the lesson. If she did not like this mute whistle, she could not be a Safe-Keeper. If she was afraid of silence, she could not learn her mother's trade. "Thank you very much," she said distinctly. "I will treasure my kirrenberry flute forever."

Now he smiled at her, more amused than she had expected. "I was sure you would," he said. "Now, I'm about ready for more of that pie—how about you?"

Chapter Two

I t was going on toward midnight before the last of the birthday guests left. Greg had fallen asleep on a blanket by his grandmother's chair, but Reed was still parading around the back lawn, his new whistle held to his mouth, producing unheard music for an invisible audience. Elminstra sighed and pushed herself to her feet.

"Well, I'm the last one here. I'd better be getting back," she said. "Greg! Wake up, child, we have a little walk home."

"He can sleep on the floor in the big room," Damiana offered.

Elminstra snorted. "You've got a houseful already," she said. "He can wake up long enough to stumble a quarter mile down the road. Greg! Gregory! Open your eyes!"

But Greg snored on. The women laughed. "I'll carry him," Thomas said, and scooped the sleeping boy into his arms. Greg never woke. "I'll be back in a little bit," he said to Damiana, and walked off with Elminstra into the soft dark.

Damiana stood up. "Reed! Fiona! Time for bed!"

For Fiona, this was the best part of the day. Every day.

She cleaned herself up at the sink in the kitchen, then hurried up the open stairs to her room. She was dressed in her nightclothes and under a light sheet when her mother came into the room, holding a single candle. Her mother settled on the edge of the bed and patted the covers around Fiona's shoulders.

"All tucked in? All comfy?"

Fiona nodded, tangling her hair on the pillow. Damiana smoothed the loose curls from her forehead, her hand cool as spring rain. "So what made today special?" she asked, as she always asked.

"A lot of things, today," Fiona said. "All the people. All the food! All the presents. Angeline."

"Turning one year older," her mother suggested.

"I don't *feel* a whole year older," Fiona said.

Damiana smiled. "No. You never do, on your birthday. On your birthday you feel exactly the same as you did the day before and the day before. Six months from now you'll feel older. In two years you'll feel older than you do right now. But it's slow. It's an invisible process."

"Like summer," Fiona said. "One day it's just there."

Damiana laughed. "Exactly like summer. And then, eventually, like winter. But not for a few months yet."

"How long will Angeline stay this time?"

"Just two or three nights, I think."

"And Thomas?"

"Maybe a week. I don't know."

"He made us whistles from kirrenberry branches."

"And have you forgiven him yet?"

Fiona scowled. "I don't have to forgive him. I don't even have to like him."

"No, you don't," her mother agreed. "Many people don't like Truth-Tellers. But if you don't like him, it should be for something he's done other than tell the truth."

"He said I wouldn't be a Safe-Keeper!" Fiona burst out.

Damiana leaned down and kissed her on the forehead. "Ah, see, he was practicing the wrong skills when he said that," she murmured. "He was pretending he could forecast what is to come. But his talent is for telling the truth, not telling the future."

"So then he doesn't know? I will be a Safe-Keeper after all?"

Damiana kissed her on the forehead again. "You will be whatever you want to be," she said, as she had said that day.

"But don't the sons and daughters of Safe-Keepers always become Safe-Keepers? Like you and Angeline did, like your mother did, like *her* mother did—"

"Many times they do. Not always. Think how dull it would be if you knew, from the very day you were born, what you would grow up to be. If everybody knew. You might become, instead, a farmer. Or an ale-maker. Or a farrier. Or a woman who raises rabbits in her hutch out back. You might become a Truth-Teller or—who knows?—the Dream-Maker. You might not want to be a Safe-Keeper after all."

Fiona picked at her mother's sleeve. "Reed can become

31

whatever he wants," she said. "He's not a Safe-Keeper's son."

Damiana laughed. "Yes, indeed, Reed does not seem like the type to sit at home and look after other people's secrets."

"I used to worry," Fiona said. "When I was little."

"Worry about what?"

"That you wouldn't love Reed as much as you loved me. Because he wasn't truly your son."

"But I do. I love you both exactly the same much," Damiana said, laughing a little at her own choice of words.

Fiona nodded solemnly. "But I didn't know that. I was little. I thought there was only so much love."

"Love is like water from the ocean," Damiana said. "You cannot empty it dry. Take bucket after bucket of water out of the Cormeon Sea, and there is still more water left than you could ever use up. That's what love's like."

"And you won't ever send him away? To Wodenderry?"

Damiana smoothed her hair away again. "Not to Wodenderry or anywhere else," she said. "Reed will only leave here if he wants to go."

Fiona turned to her side and snuggled deeper into the pillow. She was tired, but she wasn't sleepy. She thought she might lie awake a long time, thinking over the events of the day. "It was a very good party," she said.

Damiana kissed her on the ear, making her giggle. "Good night, Safe-Keeper's daughter," she whispered. "Sweetest dreams."

Damiana stood and carried her candle across the hall to

Reed's room, leaving Fiona's room in darkness. Fiona listened, as she listened every night, to her mother's goodnight interlude with Reed. They talked over the party (his favorite part of the day was playing ring-toss with Greg) and discussed which of his toys he might play with first in the morning. Finally, Damiana said, "Time to sleep, Safe-Keeper's son."

"I'm not sleepy," he said, as he said every night.

There was a moment's silence; Fiona knew her mother had leaned in to press her lips against Reed's cheek and forehead. "You're sleepy now," Damiana murmured. "I'm giving you magical sleeping kisses, all over your face."

"But I'm really not tired," he insisted.

"Ah! Another magical sleeping kiss."

"Can I come down and sit with you and Thomas and Angeline? If I can't fall asleep?"

"Lie here a while, and if you can't fall asleep in twenty minutes, then you can come downstairs and have a cup of tea. But you'll be sleepy because—here's one more!—I've given you all these magical sleeping kisses. Good night, Reed."

"Good night," he answered through a yawn.

He was, as he always was, asleep before Damiana was through the door.

Fiona listened to the sounds of her mother's footsteps going carefully down the stairway, and then to the sounds of talk and laughter that floated up during the next half hour. She closed her eyes and willed sleep to come, but it would not. Her mind was too busy showing her images from the day: Elminstra's laughing face, Thomas' haunted eyes, the sickly Victoria leaning back on the hard cushions of the traveling wagon. After a while she gave up and pushed back the covers. Moving as quietly as she could, she crept out of her bed and halfway down the stairs, perching on the small landing just where the stairwell curved, so that she would stay out of sight.

The big room below was filled with not only the noise of conversation but the scents of coffee and brandy and tobacco. Fiona could always tell when Thomas had come for a visit; he carried aromas that none of the women of the village brought inside. He was here often enough—every few months—and would usually stay a few days. Damiana, always serene and cheerful, was even more cheerful whenever he came in for a visit.

He was the one talking just now.

"Oh, yes, I was in Thrush Hollow two weeks ago," he said, his voice slow and sardonic. "Called there by the village busybody—and a committee of her friends—who wanted me to tell her neighbor what a filthy pig he was."

"And was he?" Angeline inquired.

"Worst sty I ever saw, that a man called a house and not a cow barn," Thomas said roundly. "Must have had fifteen dogs, all of them living in the house, as well as a handful of wild boys who seemed as likely to throw their garbage on the floor as take it out back and burn it. More likely, actually. You never smelled such a stench. And don't even ask me what the yard and garden looked like. Well, they'd been hobbling their horses inside the front gate at night, so you can guess for yourselves."

"So you told him he lived like an animal," Angeline prodded.

"Told him he was a disgrace to his family, as well as a hazard to general health, and that his sons needed schooling and his animals needed training and that his neighbors had decided, rightly, to send in a delegation to clean out his place."

"How did he respond?"

"At first he blustered, then he broke down, talked about his wife dying two years ago and how everything had slipped out of his hands. So I told him to welcome his neighbors' delegation and ask for their help, and maybe life would get better—and cleaner—from now on."

"But that wasn't the end of it, I'll wager," Damiana said in a soft voice.

He laughed. "No. Then I told the busybody neighbor lady that she fancied herself a righteous woman, but there wasn't a bone of human kindness in her, since she did nothing to aid a man so desperately in pain. And I told one of her committee friends that her husband was not, in fact, dead, but living over in Merendon with another woman. I didn't go looking for these truths just to be unpleasant, mind you, but they were there, apparent, and I was compelled to speak them."

Fiona could hear the smile in her mother's voice. "Never call a Truth-Teller to your house unless you are not afraid of the truth. For he sees things you would wish never to be discovered."

"There's a truth that came out down by Marring Cross just a week or so ago," Thomas said.

Marring Cross was only a few miles from Angeline's home of Lowford. "Really?" asked Angeline. "What was it?"

"Gold buried in the cleric's back yard. Enough of it to send his two young sons on their way in the world."

Fiona felt her eyes widen. Clerics were not supposed to marry and certainly should not have children. But Angeline's voice did not sound surprised when she answered. "Oh. Yes. They're half-brothers, aren't they, those boys?"

"Yes. Ten and twelve. Three people keeping those secrets, though it seems each woman was surprised as the other to find she was not the only love of this man's life."

"How did you know?" Fiona heard her mother ask.

"How did I know what?" Thomas replied.

"How did you know it was time to reveal this particular secret? Why did it become the province of the Truth-Teller and no longer the property of the Safe-Keeper of Marring Cross?"

"Actually, she didn't know," Angeline said. "But I did."

"But then—did you let go?" Thomas asked. "Because suddenly, one day, the knowledge was just in my head. I wandered down to Marring Cross and advised the town council to begin digging."

"It's strange," Angeline said. "You would think, being a Safe-Keeper, I would know the answer to that. Some secrets last only until the person who has told them is dead. Some secrets last until the Safe-Keeper knows it is time to repeat them. Some secrets are never revealed."

"Who killed Anya Haber?" Damiana murmured.

"Exactly!" Angeline exclaimed. "No one has ever answered that question, and I'm sure the Safe-Keeper of Thrush Hollow knew the answer before *she* died. But it was a secret that was meant to be kept."

"I have secrets that should die with me," Damiana said. "But will they? That's what I want to know. How can I make sure they don't get freed somehow after I'm gone?"

"I think the secret knows," Thomas said. "When to be a secret and when to be a truth. We're just the instruments that hear the words and keep them—or speak them."

Angeline yawned. "Well, here's a secret. I'm exhausted. I'm going to bed and sleeping for a hundred hours."

Damiana sounded amused. "Not with my children in the house. You'll be awake at dawn."

"Then I'd better start sleeping now."

There was the sound of chairs scraping back and dishes being gathered up. Fiona scurried back up the stairs before anyone could spot her and returned to her bed. Now she was yawning; the illicit little excursion had finally tired her out. She closed her eyes and slept.

Reed crept into her room early in the morning. "Fiona! Are you awake? Are you awake? Fiona!"

"What?" she grumbled, turning over to look at him. It was hard to remember a morning in her life that had not begun with Reed interrupting her dreaming.

"Get dressed. Come out and play," he commanded.

"I don't like ring-toss," she said with a pout.

"Not ring-toss, then! We can play war with my new soldiers. Or build my new kite. Or run down to the spring and catch fish."

"We never catch fish."

"But we will today! Or we can go down to Elminstra's and see if Greg can come out. Or we can—"

She wanted to cover her head with the pillow, but it would do no good. Reed would keep inventing alternatives until he hit upon one she liked or she wearied of telling him no. So she climbed out of bed and put on her clothes and tied her hair back in a sloppy braid. A quick, quiet trip to the kitchen, and they were on their way before anyone else in the house was astir.

They decided, after all, to go to the spring, half a mile away and icy cold no matter what the season. As always, Fiona loped along in a relatively straight line toward the goal, while Reed ranged around her in elliptical circles. He ran ahead of her to chase a butterfly, fell behind to study an anthill, tossed a ball in the air and then had to run after it when it did not land where he expected. Occasionally he would loop back to show her some treasure—a red rock, a broken flower, a captured spider with long, thin legs. Fiona was the only girl she knew who didn't mind spiders—or any other bugs, for that matter—so she inspected the creature closely and then set it free. Reed had already forgotten it, running off again in pursuit of other diversions.

When they made it to the creek, Fiona hitched up her skirts while Reed rolled up the pants of his trousers, and they waded in the water. The stones under their feet were slippery with moss, and of assorted sizes, so it was hard to keep their balance; but they were good at this. They had spent a lot of time in the creek. Fiona found three flat rocks and skipped them, one by one, down the length of the water. Reed went splashing after fish, never quiet enough or quick enough to catch them.

"When I grow up, I'm going to get a boat and go out to sea off the Cormeon coast," he announced. "And then I'll catch all the fish I want."

He was always changing his mind about what he wanted to be when he reached the age to choose a career.

"When I grow up, I'm going to stay right here," Fiona said. She had waded out of the water and was now sitting on the muddy bank, shredding long pieces of grass with her fingernails.

Reed came over with great splashing steps and she drew back a little to avoid getting spattered. He stood in the cold water right in front of her, kicking at the ripples of the current. "Or I might go to Movington and work in the mines," he said.

Fiona wrinkled her nose. "It seems like hard labor. And dirty."

"Or I might learn to be a blacksmith. Ned said he'd take me on some day, if I could ever learn to settle down."

Fiona laughed. "Then you'll never be a blacksmith."

"Or I might go to Wodenderry and meet the king," he said.

Fiona threw her scraps of grass into the swift-moving water. "I don't think it's so easy to meet the king," she said.

"I'll go up to him and say, 'Hello, your royal highness, did you know I'm your son?'"

"And he'll say, 'Here are the keys to my kingdom!'" Fiona said. "I don't think so."

"He might not think I'm really his son," Reed agreed.

"You don't have any proof."

"And Mother and Angeline will never say for sure."

"Maybe you're not the king's son," Fiona said. "Maybe you're the king's brother's son. Maybe you're the king's enemy's son. Maybe you're the son of nobody in particular, but the king's Safe-Keeper stole you out of the royal city for reasons of his own."

Reed stooped down to scoop a stone out of the water. "Well, it would be good to know for sure," he said, and skipped the stone down the stream. He was better at this than she was; it dipped in and out of the water six times before it finally sank.

Fiona shrugged. "It doesn't matter to me. I don't need to know."

"You're not curious, like I am," he said, nodding.

She shrugged again. "I don't mind secrets."

That wasn't true, though. It was just that she didn't mind this particular mystery. Other secrets made her edgy. She didn't like it when girls at the schoolhouse whispered to each other and then looked around the room and giggled and whispered some more. She didn't like it when people stopped at her mother's house looking pale and despairing, and her mother sent the children away for an hour. When Fiona and Reed returned, her mother usually looked tranquil as always, but now and then she looked troubled, a

40

little grim, as if she had eaten something that made her a bit sick. Fiona didn't like those secrets.

She had secrets of her own, things she had told no one. She had found a gold coin on the road one day, apparently dropped from a noble's coach, and she had hidden this in a little box at the bottom of her dresser. She had flirted with Calbert Seston one day out behind the schoolhouse, but he had not seemed to be aware that she was flirting and he never paid any more attention to her than he had before. She had heard Thomas say to her mother one night, "There's one truth you ought to know, and that's that I love you." And though she wished it wasn't true, her mother had replied, "I love you," right back to him. Fiona hadn't told anyone of that overheard conversation, not even Angeline, not even Reed.

Despite her ability to keep her own counsel, Fiona found that not many people confided in her. The girls at school did not draw her aside to whisper about the boys they liked or the little transgressions they had committed. Strangers did not stop her on the street so they could pour their hearts out to her. She had mentioned this to her mother, and Damiana had tried hard not to burst out laughing.

"Oh, sweetie," Damiana had said, hugging her tightly, "it doesn't work that way. You're not a Safe-Keeper when you're ten years old. You might be eighteen, you might be twenty—one day it will happen and you will just feel it. Like the silence that comes after all the crickets and the cicadas have stopped singing. You will feel it, and everyone else will sense it. But it won't happen for a while yet, if it ever does.

Listen to all the music of the world for a while yet, while you can still sing it back."

It was only Reed, really, who told her any secrets at all, and they were small ones so far. He'd accidentally broken the weather vane at Dirk's father's tavern; on purpose, he and Greg had thrown eggs at Ned's blacksmithing barn. Fiona rather disapproved of the egg-throwing incident, but she realized a Safe-Keeper could not be a judge, so she did not reprimand him. She merely said, "I'll never be the one to tell." It was Greg who confessed to his mother, which got both the boys in trouble, and they had to spend the whole next weekend cleaning out Ned's tool shed. Fiona supposed that was more a punishment for wrongdoing than for choosing the wrong confidante, and she didn't consider it her fault that the whole tale came to light. Nonetheless, it showed her the consequences of a secret betrayed, and so she vowed to guard her own private information—when she had it—with a fierce and unbreakable reserve. She thought even Thomas could not ask her to do better than that.

Chapter Three

Both Thomas and Angeline stayed two more days, then headed back to Lowford with Robert and Victoria. Three days later, the Dream-Maker came to the door.

She arrived at the house in a ramshackle traveling coach pulled by sorry, mismatched horses, and she climbed out with all the painstaking slowness of an old woman burdened by too much weight and too many aches. She was trying to pay the driver—who steadfastly refused to take her money—when Fiona and Reed came running up to throw themselves at her.

"Isadora!" they cried, frisking around her until she opened her arms and took them each into a hug.

"Look at you, Fiona, so pretty. Reed, how did you get so tall? I swear, you are two of the most beautiful children I've ever seen. Give me a hug, now, and then let me go. Reed, can you carry my bags? Goodness, you'll be a man before I know it."

Damiana came out of the house with her widest smile on

her face. Fiona knew that, of all her friends, Damiana loved Isadora the best. But then, so many people did.

"Isadora! I didn't know we were expecting you," Damiana said, leaning forward to kiss the older woman on the cheek.

"I wanted to come for the children's birthday, but I was held up in Thrush Hollow," Isadora said in a mournful voice.

Damiana instantly looked concerned. "Oh no. What's wrong?"

Isadora shook her head. "The baby—born too soon—well, that's another one gone. I stayed with my daughter two weeks, but after a while it was clear she wanted the house to herself. So I came here."

Damiana took Isadora's arm and drew her toward the door. "Fiona, can you go pick some fresh mint?" she asked over her shoulder. "I'll make some tea and we'll talk."

As Fiona moved through the herb garden, she reflected on Isadora's sad life. It was said that every Dream-Maker experienced excessive personal tragedy, but Fiona found it hard to believe that any of the other women could have gone through quite the series of calamities that Isadora had experienced before the role of Dream-Maker fell to her. She had been married quite young and had two children; her husband had died of fever. A second husband, by whom she had another child, had been hanged for murder. Fiona wasn't sure what had happened to the third husband, though he appeared to be gone for good after leaving her with three more children. Her two oldest boys had perished at sea; her youngest daughter had run away when she was fourteen and had never been seen again. This middle daughter, with whom Isadora was closest, had given birth to three stillborn children. Parents, siblings, cousins—all had either turned away from Isadora in anger or been lost to disaster.

But that was the life of a Dream-Maker, Fiona knew. Unlike Truth-Tellers and Safe-Keepers, who could be found throughout the kingdom, only one Dream-Maker lived at any given time. She was almost always an older woman whose own life had been full of woe, but everywhere she went, somebody's dearest wish came true. Thus she was beloved from one end of the kingdom to the other. Innkeepers gave her their grandest rooms; poor farmers and rich merchants pressed food and coins into her hands. Young girls showered her with kisses, hoping her mere presence could make some favored young man turn to them and fall in love.

Fiona had asked Isadora once why she decided to grant some wishes and not others. Isadora had shaken her head, and her untidy mass of gray curls had tumbled free from its pins. "I'd like to be able to tell you that," she said a little sadly. "There are so many wishes I would have granted if I could! But the power doesn't seem to work that way. It is my presence, not my will, that knocks some hidden desire into being. I have no control over the process at all."

Once that was explained, Fiona hadn't bothered to voice her own most secret wish. She just hugged it to herself and wondered if the day might arrive when the Dream-Maker's presence might make her own dream come true.

Reed was out somewhere playing—of course—but Fiona sat at the table like an adult, sipping fresh mint tea and listening to the two women talk. For a while, in hushed tones, they discussed Isadora's daughter.

"I do wonder, sometimes, if she'd be better off if I never went back to visit her," Isadora said at last. "It seems tragedy strikes her most deeply every time I'm there."

"That can't be true," Damiana said quietly. "Perhaps she is being groomed to take on your role after you're gone. Her sorrows are her own, and not of your doing."

Isadora sighed heavily. Everything about her was heavy, from her shape to her spirits to her voice; and yet her broad, sad face was the kindest one Fiona had ever seen. "I would not wish the role on anyone that I loved *or* hated," she said. "But I must confess, I am growing weary. In a few years, I will be happy enough to lay this burden down."

"Then who will be Dream-Maker after you?" Fiona asked.

The women looked over at her, both of them smiling. "I don't know," Isadora said. "But someone will step forward—someone whose life has been a study in loss. One day she will realize that, even though she still cries, someone around her is rejoicing. That though she suffers, she has the power to bring joy. Almost, it will make up to her for her own troubles."

"What dreams have you had a hand in bringing to life these past few months?" Fiona's mother asked.

"That boy in Movington—the blind one—woke up the day after I'd been there, and he could see."

"That's marvelous!" Damiana exclaimed.

"His father sent me the most beautiful shawl. I would have returned it—because, really, it was not of my doing—but I've learned by now that joy must find an expression. No one will take their gifts back. So I put it away to give to a granddaughter some day."

"What other dreams?" Fiona asked.

"Oh, a whole range of them. A merchant in Cranfield made an excellent investment with a high return. A woman in Lowford bore living twins after five stillbirths. A young man in Thrush Hollow was successful in his courtship—though I truly don't think I had a hand in that, because he was a very handsome boy," Isadora added. "I'd have accepted him myself if he'd come wooing me!"

They all laughed. "Haven't you been in the royal city for a little while?" Damiana asked.

Isadora nodded. "It's an odd place, though. So full of people, so rife with dreams and desires. I can feel them pressing at me when I walk down the streets. Some people will run after me and catch at my clothes and pour out their hopes and wishes. Other people will come to my rooms at all hours, night or day, desperate for favors. It is a very exhausting place to be."

"I wouldn't like such a place," said Fiona.

"No, and I didn't stay long," Isadora agreed. "But I felt a compulsion of sorts to go there. I don't know if there was a particular person who needed me. I don't know if I did that person any good."

"Did you see King Marcus?" Fiona asked.

Isadora nodded. "And his daughter. From a distance, of course. They were riding through the streets in a very formal procession, and there were guards all around them, so I didn't get a very good look."

"What was he like?" Damiana asked curiously.

Isadora wrinkled her nose. "I thought he appeared quite disagreeable," she said frankly. "He sat very straight on his horse and looked out over the crowd as if he was trying to smile but he didn't have much experience with smiles, so he wasn't sure how to do it. Now and then he'd lift his hand and wave, but you could tell he didn't really want to. People cheered him, of course, but I do have to wonder if they really love him."

"He's a good king," Damiana observed. "The roads are well mended, the taxes are fair, and there hasn't been war since his father was on the throne. Maybe we don't need someone warm as long as we have someone competent."

"Maybe," Isadora said rather doubtfully.

"Did he look like Reed?" Fiona asked.

Isadora laughed. "Not at all. He and his daughter are both dark, though she at least has a fair complexion. His is swarthy as a farmer's."

"Princess Lirabel," Damiana said. "What's she like? Isn't she all grown up now? Eighteen, at least?"

"Twenty," Isadora replied. "She had a more pleasant face than her father, but she looked sad. I don't know why I say that, because she was smiling and waving with much more energy than he was. But I just thought she looked unhappy."

"Perhaps her father has arranged an unwelcome marriage for her," Damiana guessed.

"I didn't hear any talk like that while I was in Wodenderry," Isadora said. "The rumor going around was that she wanted her father to acknowledge her as his heir next year, on her twenty-first birthday. But he will not do so—at least, this is what people were saying. I wasn't at court, you understand, and no one was confiding in me."

"Why won't he acknowledge her?" Fiona asked.

The older women exchanged glances. "They say he doesn't want a woman on the throne," Isadora said. "You know, he married again last year, practically the minute Lirabel's mother was dead. His new queen is quite a young woman, but so far she hasn't borne him any children. Daughters *or* sons."

"I'll bet there's someone who would have been wishing hard for your services if she'd known you were in town," commented Damiana. "The new queen."

"Perhaps I should go back soon," the Dream-Maker said with a trace of humor, "and introduce myself at the royal palace. I could live quite a life of luxury while I tried to do a favor for my king."

"Maybe that's why you felt compelled to go there after all," Damiana said. "Maybe in a few months we'll hear good news from the palace."

Isadora gave an unladylike snort. "The man's been through two wives and who knows how many companions," she said. "And he's only fathered the one child who lived to adulthood. That girl that he won't allow to succeed him to the crown."

"And Reed," Fiona piped up.

Again, the women exchanged startled glances. "There's

49

no proof that Reed is the king's son," Damiana said gently.

"You don't need proof," Fiona said. "You *know*."

"What I know might not be good enough for the king," her mother responded. "Anyway, I'm sure the king would insist upon a legitimate heir. And so far Princess Lirabel is the only one he's got."

Just then, Reed burst through the door, covered in mud and holding a coiling snake between his hands. "Look what I found in the garden!" he exclaimed. "Do we have a box where I can keep him?"

Isadora emitted a little shriek and fell back in her chair, fanning herself with her hand. Fiona hopped up to get a closer look at the sleek, sinuous body. Damiana smiled faintly.

"Well, let me just look for a box, and then I'll get dinner on the table," she said. "Isadora, it looks like *Reed's* dearest wish has come true. Now you won't have to wonder why you came to Tambleham after all."

After dinner, Reed and Fiona did the dishes, though Fiona felt that she was doing more than her share. Reed kept dropping his drying cloth so he could go inspect his new pet and see if it had eaten its own dinner of crickets and ladybugs. Damiana moved between them, humming a little, preparing gallons of tea, loaves of fresh bread, and platters of cookies, as if she expected company.

Sure enough, one by one, the neighbors started to arrive. Elminstra was first, her one-year-old granddaughter in her arms. "Isadora, I thought that was you!" she said, greeting the Dream-Maker with a kiss. "Tell me what you've seen in your travels."

"Hello, Elminstra, how good to see you," Isadora replied.

They had only exchanged a few words before the farmer down the road arrived with his two teenaged daughters, shy and beautiful. Next it was Dirk and his father; after that, the blacksmith, then the carter, then the money-changer. After that, Fiona lost track. She helped her mother bring out trays of food and gather up the used dishes, offering unobtrusive hospitality. Though all of these people had, at some point, come to this very house to seek Damiana's services, none of them were here tonight to confer with the Safe-Keeper. They were here with sincere expressions of goodwill and well-being, but they had an agenda that was nobody's secret—they hoped some of the Dream-Maker's magic would rub off on them or those they loved. None of them said so, of course. They talked of the weather, the conditions of the road, last year's harvest, next spring's fair. Most of them brought some kind of small token to press into Isadora's hand—a glittering crystal stone, a braided leather belt, a pair of embroidered slippers. Thoughtful remembrances that said in turn, *Keep me in your thoughts. When the power takes hold of you again, remember me.*

It was past midnight before all the guests were gone, and Fiona was yawning over the sink. Reed, who was not about to go up to bed even if he didn't feel like being useful, was shuffling and reshuffling a dog-eared card deck, trying to teach himself a trick. Damiana wiped down the kitchen table one last time and peered into the big main room.

51

"I think they're all gone, for the moment," Isadora said.

"Then let me fix up the bed for you," Damiana said. "You two—go on upstairs. I'll be there in a minute."

Reed, of course, protested, but without much credibility. Fiona washed her face and went upstairs without another word. She tried, as always, to listen to the adult conversation transpiring below, but she was too tired. She fell asleep before her mother had even come upstairs to kiss her good-night.

Chapter Four

At first, it seemed like nothing in particular came of Isadora's visit. No one found gold in his back yard in the week after she'd left; no extraordinary babies were born. Classes were not miraculously canceled, so Fiona and Reed trudged out to the schoolhouse every day, kicking their way through the first curled brown leaves of early autumn. Fiona did not suddenly with a touch of the Dream-Maker's hand understand the intricacies of math; and Calbert Seston did not seem to have any greater awareness of her existence. Her deeper, darker wishes, of course, did not come true—but then, neither did anybody else's.

Until Madeleine Herbrush's mother died two weeks after the Dream-Maker left town.

Madeleine, a pretty, reserved girl about four years older than Fiona, hadn't been at school that day, but Fiona hadn't particularly remarked on that. The schoolhouse was small enough to have only two rooms and two teachers. Just this fall, Fiona and Reed had been moved up to the room where the ten- to sixteen-year-olds were taught, and Madeleine was in this classroom, though she was often absent. Many of the students were. The farmers' children had duties at planting and harvest times; children from large families were frequently required to stay home and help their mothers take care of sick siblings or handle other chores. Damiana was a firm believer in education, and so she rarely succumbed to any arguments that Fiona or Reed put forward when they tried to convince her that they needed a day off from school. But they were among the few who could be found regularly in the schoolhouse.

It was only after she got home that Fiona heard the news. Reed had skipped alongside her down the road to home, then continued on toward Elminstra's to see if Greg was available to play. Elminstra herself was seated in the Safe-Keeper's kitchen, sipping tea. Damiana stood with her back against the cabinets, holding her own steaming mug. She wore that expression that Fiona liked least—the one where she tried to show no expression at all.

"What's going on?" Fiona said, because clearly something was.

Her mother tried a smile. "Hello, sweet girl. How was your day?"

"It was all right. I didn't do so badly in math. What's wrong?"

"Birdie Herbrush died last night. We're talking about what we might do for her family," Damiana said.

Fiona was instantly sorry. "Madeleine's mother? Oh, the poor thing! Doesn't she have three little brothers and sisters? And a father that travels all the time?"

Damiana nodded tightly. Elminstra said, "Well, I hate to see anybody leave school before they're done, but she just might have to. Stay home and take care of those younger ones."

"Her sister's thirteen," Damiana said. "Old enough to be some help when their father's gone."

Elminstra made a sympathetic noise. "Still. Four children and no mother. It's got to be a nightmare for Dale Herbrush."

"Well, it's a dream come true for Madeleine—for all the children in that house," Damiana said quietly. "Isadora's visit did some good after all."

For a moment, no one in the kitchen spoke. Damiana had said the words so calmly that they didn't instantly register; and when they did, both Fiona and Elminstra stared at her.

"What do you mean," Fiona said, "a dream come true?"

But Elminstra had figured it out more quickly than a ten-year-old would. "Oh, my," said the older woman, shaking her head and gazing down at the table. "Oh, my lord. Once in a while I thought—and there would be those bruises—but I thought, well, children play. They fall, they get hurt. I suppose this was a secret you've been keeping a while?"

"Five years," Damiana said.

"What secret? What are you talking about?" Fiona demanded, though she had already guessed part of the answer. Why would any child be happy to learn that her mother had died? Fiona shivered and hoped, just a little, that her mother would tell her this was one of those things

55

she was too young to know. But her mother looked straight at her and replied.

"Madeleine's mother was a violent woman. She would go into rages and beat her children—Madeleine—all of them," Damiana said. "And Madeleine was afraid to tell anyone, because her mother had threatened to do more harm to her brother and sisters if she did. One day Madeleine came home from school to find the other three children tied to the door and bleeding. She stayed so she could protect them—and she told no one for the same reason."

Fiona felt her lips trembling as she tried to shape the words. "But she—she told *you*," she whispered.

Damiana moved her shoulders in a gesture that might have been a shrug. "She had to tell someone," she said. "And I could keep her secret safe."

Elminstra looked up at last. "But you need not keep it any longer? She does not fear the pity they will all receive when the story is told?"

Damiana shook her head. "She said she wanted the world to know that her mother was a cruel woman."

"She had a lot of friends here," Elminstra said hesitantly. "You are the Safe-Keeper, of course, but will everyone believe you?"

Damiana smiled somewhat grimly. "If they do not, I will call Thomas to town. No one disputes him."

Fiona had listened to these last few exchanges in silence, feeling like her head was about to burst open. "But how could you!" she finally exclaimed. "How could you keep such a secret?"

Her mother looked at her with eyes as shadowed as ever Thomas's could be. "Because that's what I do," she said gently. "Keep secrets."

"But not such dreadful ones!"

"Sometimes," Damiana said, still in that gentle voice. "I know secrets that are worse than this one."

"But you—but you—but things like that should be *told!*"

"Maybe," her mother replied. "But not by me."

Fiona shook her head. Inside, it felt like her brain was buzzing with a convocation of angry bees. "But surely Madeleine came to you because she thought you could help her—"

Elminstra looked over at her. "It was a help. You don't know it yet, but sometimes the weight of knowledge is almost too much to bear. Sharing it with one other living soul is enough to ease your burden. Even if no one else ever learns of it. Even if nothing changes."

Fiona shook her head again, more violently, but she could not dislodge the bees. "I don't understand," she said fiercely. "How could you not have done anything to help her?"

"Fiona—" her mother said, but Fiona flung her mug to the floor. It exploded into a dozen pieces and threw liquid in as many directions. Fiona ran through the door and down the lawn and out toward the streambed, without pausing to see if anyone hurried after her or even came to the door and called out her name.

She spent the next two hours sitting on the bank of the spring, watching the water gurgle past. The air was still hot enough, this early in the season, to make the notion of wading in cold water seem pleasant, but she hadn't bothered to unlace her shoes and step in. She hadn't bothered to undo the top two buttons of her dress, which she usually did as soon as she got home. She hadn't bothered to pick up a stone and bounce it down the glittering surface of the water. She just sat there and stared, and wondered how soon the world would fall apart.

Reed came looking for her around the dinner hour. She heard him coming from fifty feet away, because he was making no effort at stealth, but he did not call to her. He didn't even greet her when he arrived at the streambed. He merely dropped to a seat beside her on the muddy bank and put his arm around her waist.

They sat there a few moments in silence, and the only thing in the whole world that seemed to have direction or motion was the creek before them. As a rule, Reed was not formed for quiet, but on rare occasions, when the situation demanded, he could sit still as a cat watching an unwary bird. That was how he sat now while Fiona continued to watch the water.

Finally she sighed and stirred. His arm tightened briefly, and then he released her. He pulled his kirrenberry whistle out of his pocket and began blowing silent melodies into the hushed twilight.

"I couldn't have kept a secret like that," Fiona said at last.

Reed held the whistle up to his eye and peered down it as if wondering what obstruction kept its voice silent. "You didn't have to," he said. "It wasn't told to you."

58

"But someday, when I'm a Safe-Keeper, someone will tell me a story like that. I don't know what I'll do."

"You don't have to be a Safe-Keeper," he said.

"But I want to be."

He shrugged and put the whistle away. Finding a handful of round stones, he dropped them one by one into the racing current. "Then you'll learn the way of it. Someday. But there's no reason you have to start practicing now."

"What if I'm never good enough?" she asked, not looking at him.

He balanced a bigger rock on his head a moment, then jerked forward with enough force that it flew away from him and into the stream. "Well, I suppose, you tell somebody's secret, and nobody ever tells you secrets again, and then you get a different job," he said. "Ned said he tried to be a carpenter before he was a blacksmith, but he could never understand the wood. He says he understands iron."

"It's not the same thing," she said impatiently.

He shrugged and threw a rock so hard that it landed on the other side of the creek, hit a tree, and rolled into the water anyway. "I don't see why not," he said. "It's just finding out what you're good at. Most people don't know that when they're ten years old."

"All you're good at is throwing rocks," she said irritably.

He grinned over at her. His eyes were a freckled green, fringed with spiky brown lashes, and even when he was serious he looked like he was up to mischief. "What I want to know," he said, "is what some of the other secrets are."

"You can't ask that!"

"But don't you wonder? And what Angeline's secrets are? Do you think they know about buried gold? Like the cleric in Thrush Hollow had?"

"I don't know. Maybe."

"Or maybe they know that—that—Lacey stole a diamond ring from Elminstra's house."

"Elminstra doesn't have any diamond rings."

"Well, she doesn't *now*," Reed said.

Fiona couldn't keep herself from laughing. "Maybe they know where old Josh keeps his still."

"Maybe they know about people who've been *murdered*."

"No! That's terrible!"

"Bad people," Reed said quickly. "People who deserved to die."

For a moment, Fiona heard the echo of her mother's voice. *Who killed Anya Haber?* "They probably know who killed them," she said, entering into the spirit of it, "and how they did it, and why."

"They might be hiding evidence," Reed said. "A knife. Or a cup of poison."

Fiona glanced over her shoulder. "Maybe," she breathed, "they helped bury the bodies."

Reed leaned over to whisper in her ear. "Maybe," he said, "there's one buried in our root cellar."

Fiona shrieked and covered her ears, but now she was laughing. "No! I won't be able to sleep tonight!"

"Fi-o-na," Reed moaned in an unearthly voice. "I'm coming back to find my bones."

She screamed again and scrambled to her feet. Reed chased her all the way home, crooning her name and making her laugh so hard she almost couldn't keep her footing.

That night, Fiona was under the covers with one candle still lit when Damiana came in to tuck her into bed. Her mother sat on the edge of the mattress and brushed her blond hair back, as always.

"So are you still upset with me?" her mother asked.

Fiona stared up at her, trying to read secrets on the smooth, composed face. She wondered if this was why Damiana always seemed so untroubled, no matter how hectic the day; she knew of so much that was so much worse. "I'm trying to understand it," she said at last.

"Everybody has a part to play," her mother said. "Bart Seston raises cattle, the butcher slaughters them so we can have food. A midwife brings people into the world, an undertaker buries them when they die. Life is good sometimes, hard sometimes, bad sometimes, and good again."

"I don't always understand your part," Fiona said.

"I am the voice that says 'I know' when someone tells me 'This is too hard for me to hold on to by myself.' I am the soul who reminds other souls that they are not alone. I cannot bring them solutions, I cannot make their troubles disappear, I can only say that I hear them and I understand. Sometimes that's enough."

"Sometimes it's not," Fiona said.

"Sometimes it's not," her mother agreed. "And then they look for help from someone other than me."

"You said you knew other secrets, even ones worse than Madeleine's."

Damiana was quiet for a moment. "One or two," she said at last.

Fiona shook her head against the pillow. "But aren't they ever too much for *you* to know?" she asked.

"Sometimes. Sometimes I have to hear someone say 'I know' when I have a secret too great to hold on to in silence. And then I tell Angeline. Or the Safe-Keeper in Thrush Hollow. Someone else who understands silence."

"You can't tell Thomas, though."

"Thomas is the last one I would tell."

"It's strange that the two of you would be friends, then."

Damiana smiled. "Ah, but Thomas is my mirror image, don't you see? Or perhaps it is stronger than that. He brings light where I create darkness. He gets to say aloud all the things I have kept to myself. When the time for secrets is past, and the time for truth has arrived."

Fiona turned on her side and folded her hands together under her chin. "I think it would be hard," she said. "To hide the truth or to tell it. It would be so hard."

Damiana leaned down and kissed her on the cheek. "Any task worth doing is."

Chapter Five

hat fall, Fiona's greatest secret was that she was desperately in love with Calbert Seston. He was two years older than she was, a swaggering, honey-blond farmer's son with an angular face and the well-developed muscles of a laborer. He could beat up any boy in the schoolhouse, both older and younger, and he had a fine, defiant way of answering Miss Elmore when she asked him a question in class. All the girls in the second classroom blushed and sighed when he looked their way, but he was not much interested in girls. He would rather win a footrace from the quarter-mile marker to the schoolhouse door than spend five minutes making conversation with the prettiest girl in class. Even Megan Henshaw, who was fourteen and beautiful, could not hold his attention for long, though it was an accepted thing that they were destined to marry. Megan's father owned a slaughterhouse near the Seston property, and Calbert's father owned the biggest herd of cattle for miles around. Megan was bored and possessive when Cal was sitting near her, familiar with him through years of family dealing and somewhat blinded to his magnetism. But she knew all the other girls adored him, and so she wanted him, and made sure to touch his arm or address him directly at least once a day, even when he appeared to be ignoring her.

Fiona told no one, but she was sure, she had a preternatural certainty, that she and Calbert Seston were destined to be together. Everything about him appealed to her, from the shape of his face to the stance of his body. She would grin to herself when he made some obscure comment that no one else in the room, not even Miss Elmore, understood, because *she* had understood it; it had seemed clever to her. She knew his wardrobe by heart. She could often guess, half an hour before he arrived at school in the morning, whether he would be wearing his blue shirt or the plain cotton white one with the tiny tear by the collar. She could distinguish his voice in any group, no matter how many were talking at once or how far down the road they might be. His laugh delighted her. His smile haunted her. She wanted to be with him forever.

Often she was amazed at how well they had been designed for each other. His father's farm—which Cal, an only child, would inherit—was situated just outside of town on the northern edge. It was private enough for someone who wanted to consult with a Safe-Keeper, but close enough to town that it was not hard to reach. His steady income from farming and raising cattle would mean she would not have to worry when troubled visitors arrived at her door, whispering, "I cannot pay you. I have nothing to give." And since farming was a job that took a man's time, often from sunup till sundown, Fiona would be alone enough to make visitors feel comfortable about creeping in to tell their secrets.

They were truly meant for each other, although Calbert did not seem to know it yet.

Fiona sometimes thought she should wait till they were both much older—eighteen and sixteen, perhaps—before she let him know how much she loved him and how well suited they were. But then she worried that some other girl might snatch him up first—Megan Henshaw, most likely, because all you had to do was look at her smooth, scheming face and know that she was already planning her wedding down to the last fall of lace. Therefore, most of the time Fiona thought she should tell him now, as soon as she could, so he realized where his future lay and began to prepare for it. Even so, she might not have approached him that day in late autumn except that circumstances combined to put them alone together for a few moments, and Fiona seized the opportunity when she had it.

It had not, on the face of it, been a propitious day. Cal had arrived late that morning, sauntering in with a little half-sneer on his face, nodding in acknowledgment when his friends greeted him with whistles and cheers. Miss Elmore, who had been outlining a mathematical problem to the ten- and eleven-year-olds, did not at first respond to his arrival, just finished her long explanation. Fiona reacted, though; her breath caught slightly in her throat and her heart fluttered a moment behind her ribs. From the corner of her eye, she watched Cal take his seat, stretch out his long legs before him, and toss out a laughing comment to his admirers.

Miss Elmore was still talking. "Very well. I want you to solve the problems I've written on the board. No talking to each other, mind, and no cheating! Calbert," she said, almost with no change in inflection and turning casually in his direction, "what was the crisis that kept you from our presence so long this morning?"

None of the ten-year-olds began work yet on their math problems, just held their pencils suspended above their papers. Everybody in the room wanted to hear the answer to this.

"Am I late?" Cal asked outrageously, drawling the words. "Stupid rooster. It doesn't seem to know morning from night anymore."

"Blaming a farm animal. That doesn't seem right," Miss Elmore replied. "I think you need to take a little more responsibility for your own actions."

"Well, I'm responsible for feeding him. Maybe if I let him go hungry a few mornings he'll wake up a little faster."

The boys sitting around him laughed. Fiona smiled. Miss Elmore was not amused.

"Maybe if I let you sit inside for a few lunch periods you'll learn how to get here a little faster," she said.

Calbert scowled. "I'm not staying in at lunch."

Miss Elmore shrugged. "Or you can stay an hour after class for three days. Your choice."

Cal couldn't stay after class, and everyone knew it, since

66

his father required him to be home in time to help with evening chores. Cal's father actually wasn't entirely sure an education was what his boy needed, and public opinion pretty much assumed that Cal stayed in school only to spite his father. At times like these, Fiona worried that Miss Elmore's strictness might make Cal decide that working full time on the farm was better than spending half his life in class.

But Cal was too imperturbable to let on if Miss Elmore had bested him. He shrugged and settled back more comfortably in his chair. "Fine. I'll sit in at lunch. Doesn't matter to me."

"Good," said Miss Elmore briskly. "Now. While the younger children work on math, I want the rest of you to sit and listen. I'm going to read you a story written by a royal scribe in Wodenderry."

Fiona half listened to the story Miss Elmore read, but she wasn't too engaged by the tale. She put more of her attention on the arithmetic. She didn't think she had completed her addition correctly on at least three of the problems, and she wished Reed was sitting close enough so that she could surreptitiously show him her paper and he could indicate her success by a smile or a frown. But she was sitting near the back and Reed was in the front row. Miss Elmore had separated them three weeks ago for just such an infraction. So she sighed and looked over the problems again, trying to drown out the sound of Miss Elmore's voice.

Once the reading was over, the entire classroom turned to history and geography, and then they were all given writing assignments modulated by grade. Lunchtime couldn't come fast enough after that, and they all spilled out into the dirt clearing that served as their play area when they weren't trapped inside.

Fiona took her lunch with a couple of the girls in her class, eating the bread and cheese and apple that her mother had packed for her the night before. She would have preferred to eat with Reed, but he always gobbled everything down in five minutes and then ran off somewhere with his friends. She could always hear them thrashing about in the woods nearby, or yodeling out insults, or throwing things that might not have done much damage but always generated a great deal of noise.

Today she had just finished her meal when Reed materialized beside her, a long red scratch weeping blood along his forearm. "Reed! What did you do?"

"Caught it on a branch," he said, not overly concerned. "Do you have something I can wrap it with?"

"No, but Miss Elmore probably does," she said. "I'll go ask."

"That doesn't look like a branch mark. That looks like you got caught on a thorn," Fiona heard one of the other girls say.

"Do you think it's poisonous?" Reed asked. He said it as if that would please him.

Fiona didn't hear what the other girls replied because she was already inside the schoolhouse. A few steps down the hall and she was turning into the upper-grade room.

Where Miss Elmore was nowhere to be found, but Cal Seston was making his presence felt.

He was standing on a chair in front of the blackboard.

drawing naughty pictures in chalk. He spun around when he heard the door open, and then relaxed when he saw it was only Fiona. He grinned at her.

"Thought you might be the old witch," he said.

Fiona studied the illustrations, mostly crude images of naked women. The subject matter didn't offend her, but she wished he'd shown a little more artistic ability. This must be the first thing she'd come across that Cal wasn't good at. "She'll know you're the one who did it," was all she said.

"Nah. I'll tell her I fell asleep and they were on the board when I woke up. Someone trying to make me look bad."

"She won't believe you."

He shrugged. "I don't care what she thinks."

She admired that level of self-assurance; she tried not to care what people thought, but sometimes she still did. "Where did she go?"

He hopped down from the chair and was standing so close to her she could smell the soap and sweat on his body. "She didn't bother to tell me. What do you want her for?"

Reed's cut was not deep and he rarely bothered to stop for small wounds, anyway. Fiona doubted he was even still waiting for her to return to the playfield. "Oh—I had a question for her. But I'd rather talk to you," she said in a rush.

He folded his arms and leaned back against the board. "Me! I'm not good at answering questions."

She smiled at him. "Not a math question or a history question, silly. I just wanted to know if you'd ever—if you thought—if you realized—I think you and I were meant to be together."

It took a moment for him to digest the words; she watched his face change as he understood and considered them. "What do you mean, together?" he asked presently. "Like, you want me to kiss you? Go to the festivals with you? Stuff like that?"

"That would be fun," she agreed. "But I meant — forever. We were meant to get married and live together and have children and spend our lives with each other."

There was a moment of blank silence, and then he hooted with laughter. "I'm not going to marry you!" he exclaimed.

"Not now, of course," she said patiently. "But you—"

"Not ever!" he broke in. "You're a bastard child! No one is going to marry you! And you're ugly, too, with that pale face and those funny eyes. I'd give you a kiss or two if you really wanted, but I wouldn't court you for real. Nobody will. You don't have a father or a name. Or enough of a face to make up for it."

Fiona stared at him and could not speak.

He stared back at her a moment and then laughed again. "Damn," he said. "This day's getting crazier all the time." He pushed past her and walked back toward his seat.

Fiona stared at the place on the blackboard where his body had just been. It seemed to shimmer and be on the point of dissolving. Her ears seemed to be expanding and contracting, allowing sound in and then shutting it off in an uncertain rhythm. She thought there might be the sound of footsteps crossing the room, but with the unreliability of her hearing she could not be sure.

"She thought I might want to *marry* her," Cal said from behind her. So someone else must have entered the room. Fiona closed her eyes in mortification. She had thought it could not get worse, but if Calbert was going to repeat every word she said—

"I heard her," said a quiet voice.

Fiona opened her eyes. Reed. She did not turn around.

"You're a brat and a nuisance, but at least you've got royal blood in you. A man doesn't mind talking to *you*," Cal said. "But she's loony. And she's never going to get a husband, let alone me."

Reed's voice was soft, easy, the voice he used when he was fishing in earnest and didn't want to startle away his prospects. "My mom's friends with the witch down the road," he said. "Elminstra? You know her?"

"She's loony, too," Cal said.

"If I asked her to, she'd give me a potion for warts and hives. She'd give me a potion that would make your skin itch and flake off and turn bloody when you scratched it. She'd give me a potion that would make your hair fall out and never grow back. Or worse," Reed said.

There was a moment's silence.

"I didn't do anything," Cal said sullenly.

"If you ever say another word about my sister—to her, or to anybody else—I'll get every single one of those potions from Elminstra, and more besides," said Reed. "I'll put one in your milk one day, and spread one on your chair another day. I'll spill one on your head when you're walking home from school and I'm sitting up in a tree hanging over the road. If you ever say a word about my sister, or to my sister, you'll be sorry I didn't find the potion that would make you curl up on your daddy's farm and die."

This second silence was even more profound.

"I wasn't going to say anything," Cal said at last.

"Good," Reed said and walked the remaining few feet across the room till he was at Fiona's side. "Did you find something to tie up my arm?" he asked.

Still staring at the blackboard, she shook her head. Reed added, "Well, let's look for Miss Elmore, then. It's still bleeding." And he put his hand on her shoulder, turned her toward the door, and walked between her and the sight of Cal Seston until they were out of the room.

She was crying by the time they got to the hallway, and so blinded with tears that she couldn't blunder her way out the door to the dirt clearing. Reed led her in the other direction anyway, out the front door to the narrow porch overlooking the road that led away from school, back to home and safety. All of the other children were out back, so they sat together on the porch, Reed with his arm around Fiona, Fiona sobbing wretchedly.

"He said—he said—" she choked out and his arm tightened.

"I heard him," Reed replied.

"Why would anybody be so *mean*?" she wailed.

"Cal Seston's a rat and a bully. Everybody knows it. Everybody but all the girls," he added somewhat bitterly.

"But why would he *say* those things?"

"Because he likes to hurt people. Because he thinks it's funny."

72

"I'm so embarrassed," she moaned.

"He won't tell anybody."

"He will."

"He won't. Or I'll give him a rash in places where he didn't know he could itch."

Fiona giggled through a sob. "What if he didn't believe you?"

"Well, then, he'll find out, won't he?"

Fiona lifted her head, which she had burrowed into Reed's shoulder. "Don't you," she begged, "don't you tell anyone how stupid I was."

He kissed her on the cheek. "I won't," he said. "Not a word."

And he never did.

Chapter Six

They were all together again for Wintermoon, Angeline arriving in company with Thomas, and Isadora brought to the Safe-Keeper's cottage by a Cranfield merchant who had been only too happy to do a favor for the Dream-Maker. It was the most joyous holiday of the year, though it took place on the coldest, darkest day, and Fiona and her mother had been baking for days in preparation.

There were pies made from dried summer apples, and sweet hard cookies. There were three kinds of bread and two varieties of cake. They had made blackberry tarts and blueberry tarts, and Fiona had suggested they make kirrenberry tarts as well.

"Ugh. No. They have a very bitter taste," her mother had said.

"I thought we could give one to Thomas. And maybe it would turn him silent for a day," Fiona said.

Damiana choked and started laughing. "Make him some kirrenberry tea and see if he drinks it," she said through her laughter. "It would have the same effect."

But of course Fiona didn't.

Everyone arrived at once, Angeline and Thomas from the west, Isadora from the east, and they all hurried into the house to get warm. Everyone was loaded down with bundles—clothes for a few days' stay, of course, as well as the traditional gifts of the holiday—and all the travelers carried inside with them the sweet, clean scent of winter.

"My, I don't remember a winter so cold in at least ten years," Isadora exclaimed. "Poor Helwick, he'd loaded up his wagon with hot bricks for my feet, and he kept asking me if I was warm enough, but of course I wasn't. I finally snapped at him, 'Well, it would be a dream come true if the whole cart caught fire right now and I could get warm all over.' So the whole rest of the trip he kept looking around, afraid everything in the wagon was going to go up in flames."

"It wouldn't be so bad if it would snow," said Angeline.

"It would be worse!" Thomas replied. "Then it would be cold *and* wet, and your trip back to Lowford would be even slower than your trip here."

"But at least it would be pretty," Damiana said.

"Till the horses churned it up and your kids mucked it up and it melted and froze a few more times—"

"*He's* in a fine mood," Damiana observed to her sister. "Was he like this the whole way from Lowford?"

Angeline grinned. "He doesn't like the cold."

"Well, it's warm inside," Damiana said. "Everybody get your things settled in. Fiona and I will put dinner on the table."

Since the six of them had celebrated Wintermoon

75

together for as long as Fiona could remember, everyone knew exactly where their bundles belonged. Reed had already been moved to Fiona's room, to sleep on a mat on the floor; Angeline would sleep in his bed. Isadora, who claimed she could not climb stairs of any kind, would sleep on the sofa in the main room. Thomas would stow his gear in Damiana's own room, as he always did. The house would be full, but merry.

After the meal, which was delicious, they gathered in the main room to begin decorating the house. Fiona and Reed had spent the last two days roaming the woods to find the proper boughs—oak for strength, birch for beauty, cedar for serenity, evergreen for steadfastness, rowan for faith—and they had brought them all back to make a huge pile in the middle of the main room. They would weave all the branches together—the thin, bare limbs of the wood twined with the supple bright strands of evergreen—to make ropes to wind over every surface or dangle above every doorway. They would save the best branches, of course, for the big wreath that would hang over the fireplace until Wintermoon night.

The women had hoarded ribbons and scraps from sewing projects all year, and these were used to bind the branches and add their own magic and memories. "Lace from a young girl's wedding gown—that's for hope," Angeline said, dropping her contribution into the pile.

"Red ribbon from Fiona's winter dress—that's for merriment," said Damiana.

"Gold thread for riches," said Isadora.

76

"Blue silk for summer," said Fiona.

Thomas, who did most of the work of binding and hanging the branches, rarely had actual items to contribute, but this year he pulled out a long strand of twine hung with tiny brass bells. "Given to me by an unfriendly merchant who found my revelations less than appealing," Thomas said with a little smile. "He said I should always wear these wrapped like a collar around my neck, so that everyone could hear me coming and prepare."

Damiana and Angeline laughed at that, though Fiona didn't think it was so funny. Who would want to be the kind of person whose arrival made everyone apprehensive?

"What shall they represent?" Angeline asked.

Thomas raised his eyebrows at that, as if the answer "truth" was so obvious that he didn't need to state it. But Damiana took hold of the long string of bells and shook them to a sweet frenzy. "Let them stand for celebration," she said, and they all agreed.

Reed, who rarely had the patience to sit at the hearth and plait tree limbs together, had been outside in the cold dark since directly after dinner. But now he came bursting through the front door, bringing starlight and frost in with him.

"Reed! Close the door!" Isadora begged.

It slammed behind him as he came bounding up to the five of them seated on the floor. "I found it!" he panted.

Fiona and the others looked up at him. He had grown another inch the past two months and resisted getting his fair hair cut, and so he looked the very picture of a ragged, abandoned urchin. But his green eyes were alight with excitement, and he could not have looked happier. "Found what?" Angeline and Damiana asked together.

But Fiona knew. "Oh, Reed, did you?" she exclaimed, jumping to her feet. "Let me see."

He carefully unwrapped a length of blue cotton while the adults came to their feet and drew close enough to see. There, coiled in five thin circles, was a length of truelove vine, its flat, heart-shaped leaves still red from the onslaught of autumn.

"Elminstra told me she's only found it once for Wintermoon, but she looks every year," Reed said. "I knew if I looked and looked and *looked*, I'd find it sometime."

Damiana picked it delicately from his hands, and it twined around her wrist and fingers like a live thing. "I don't think I've ever found any at this time of year," she said, shaking her head. "I don't even know what it's supposed to represent on the wreath. Love? Heart's ease? Does anybody know?"

"I'll take some down to Elminstra and ask her," Fiona suggested.

"Oh, good idea. There's plenty here to share," her mother answered.

"I'll go, too," Reed said.

Fiona looked over at him. "I didn't mean *now*."

"We can't bind it into the wreaths until we know what it's for," Isadora said.

"We can finish the wreaths tomorrow," said Damiana.

But Fiona had already sighed and headed toward the

doorway, where they kept their winter boots in a somewhat muddy box. "Oh, very well, we'll go now. But I want very hot tea and a very large piece of cake when I get back."

In a few minutes, she and Reed were bundled up to their eyebrows in coats and scarves, and they were running down the road to Elminstra's. It was so cold that Fiona could feel the inside of her nose freeze; her throat filled with icicles when she breathed. Reed raced ahead of her and then ran back to make sure she was not stumbling in the frozen ruts of the road. Her fingers tingled with cold. Within five minutes, she could no longer feel her toes.

But it was not far to Elminstra's, and soon enough they were pounding on her door and tumbling inside. All was chaos at the witch's house, for it was filled with Elminstra's children and grandchildren and what might have been half a dozen friends besides. The fire burned brightly on the hearth and candles had been thrust into sconces throughout the main room, revealing piles of wood and greenery in all stages of weaving.

"Bless you, children, what are you doing out on such a night?" Elminstra demanded. "Your mother—is something wrong?"

"No, we have a Wintermoon gift for you—" Fiona started.

"And a question to ask," Reed finished.

"Take off your coats, then. Though I can't imagine what question . . . Do you want tea or hot chocolate to warm you up?"

Fiona shook her head, though Reed immediately opted for hot chocolate. Pausing only to take off his dirty boots and unwind a wool scarf from his face, Reed ran to the kitchen behind Greg and his mother.

"So what is it you've come to ask me?" Elminstra said.

Fiona handed her the square of black silk in which Damiana had wrapped about six inches of truelove vine. "If we're to tie this into our Wintermoon wreaths," she said, "what is it we're asking for?"

Elminstra gasped as she folded back the black silk and revealed the bright red leaves of the vine. Two of her daughters crowded around her to see what had amazed her. "Truelove!" Elminstra exclaimed. "Wherever did you get it? And fresh picked, too, because it's still springy and bright."

"Reed found it somewhere in the forest. We thought you should have some. But Isadora said we couldn't weave it into our wreaths until we knew what it would bring us."

Elminstra lifted it reverently from its black bed and let the curling vine insinuate itself between her fingers. "Heart's desire," she said, a little absently. "It means something different for everyone."

Fiona was a little disappointed in the answer, though she supposed it made sense. She had been hoping for something more grand from something deemed so precious. True love, for instance; shouldn't that be what was conferred by a vine with such a name? "I'll tell my mother," she said.

Reed reappeared, fortified by cocoa, winding his scarf back around his face. "Are we ready to go?" he demanded. "There's cake waiting at home."

"No wonder he just keeps growing," Elminstra said. "He just keeps eating. Reed, thank you so much for the truelove. It was kind of you to think of me."

"What's it for?" he asked.

"Your heart's desire," Fiona said.

He considered that and shrugged. "I think I already have everything I want," he said.

Elminstra laughed and patted him on the head, through the layers of wool. "That's because you're young and can't think of much to want," she said. "Trust me, the older you get, the more will come to mind."

"Come on," he said to Fiona. "Let's go home and finish the wreaths."

In fact, it was another two days before the wreaths were finished, since they kept taking breaks to do other things. Thomas insisted on chopping two months' worth of wood to stack up behind the house, though Damiana said she was perfectly capable of cutting her own logs, thank you very much. "And Reed's gotten very handy with an ax," she added.

"Reed will be bigger than I am in a few years' time, but for now, he's ten years old and I'm here," Thomas replied.

The women went visiting, taking bread and baked treats to friends and neighbors, and entertained others who dropped by the Safe-Keeper's house. Fiona went with them some of the time, and some of the time played with Reed, running through the bare-branched woods or pausing by the frozen stream. If they chipped down through the top layer of ice, they could find the running water beneath, so cold that it hurt their mouths to take a swallow. They always drank from it anyway, then shrieked with pain and delight.

On Wintermoon night itself, they ate a feast of a dinner

and drank two bottles of wine. Fiona and Reed were allowed only one glass apiece, and Fiona didn't particularly care for the taste of even that much, but she drank it anyway because it was supposed to be festive. The adults seemed to relish the rare treat, though. Angeline grew silly, and Isadora laughed as if she didn't have a single care. Thomas became much more mellow, his voice losing its sarcastic edge and his eyes their haunted shadows. Damiana did not seem to change at all, merely smiling at them all as if she loved them with her entire heart. But she always did that.

After the meal, they went outside to light the great bonfire that Thomas and Reed had built before the sun went down. The wood was dry and caught quickly, and soon they had a fierce blaze going that they would feed till dawn. Reed and Fiona climbed a nearby tree so that they could gaze some distance up and down the road and spot similar fires in Elminstra's yard and other houses even farther away.

When the fire had burned a good hour or two, Thomas went into the house and came out bearing the big wreath that had hung over the fireplace for the past two days. It was bound with all their most precious mementos—the strand of truelove, Thomas's bells, Angeline's lace—and carried with it all their hopes and dreams for the new year.

"Put it on the fire, then," Damiana said, and he tossed it on the very top of the blaze. It seemed to Fiona that for a moment there was a circle of concentrated fire within the random tongues of flame, and then the wreath seemed to crumple and disappear.

"May we have all we hoped for," Angeline said. "May we

have happiness and health and love and well-being all of next year."

"And the next," said Isadora.

"And the next," said Thomas.

"And the next," said Fiona.

"And the next," said Reed.

Damiana said nothing, just poked at the fire with the end of a thin, blackened stick. Fiona was to remember that long after this blaze fell to ashes and Summermoons came and Wintermoons came, and came and came again. Of the six of them, only five had spoken up to lay claim to happiness in the coming years. If Damiana had lifted her voice that night, would happiness have visited them a sixth year as well? Or had she remained silent because she already knew the truth and had determined to keep it a secret? The fire burned through the oak, the birch, the cedar, the truelove, the lace, the ribbon, the gold, and they all watched it, and no one chose to speak about the things that were to come.

Part

Chapter Seven

he year she was fifteen, Fiona spent much of her time learning herb lore at Elminstra's house. She had never wavered in her desire to be a Safe-Keeper, but her mother had convinced her that it was a good idea to have a steady source of income besides.

"Your aunt sews. I make fair copies of correspondence and compose letters for people who can't write," Damiana said. "There's not much money in Safe-Keeping, and it's not the sort of profession that allows you to turn people away if they can't pay you. So it's best to have a second career, one that brings in a little money, and you like the herb work. You're so good in the garden."

Fiona did, indeed, enjoy the herb work, the medicinal and sometimes almost magical properties that could be found in seed and root and petal. And she enjoyed her time with Elminstra, who was always so open and friendly, and whose house was always filled with other people.

While Fiona learned herb lore, Reed tried various apprenticeships in the village. But he was too restless to apply himself to any one of them for long. He had the strength to be a blacksmith, said Ned, but he couldn't be trusted to keep his eyes on the fire. He had an aptitude for woodmaking, said the carpenter, but at any minute he would lay down his chisel or lathe and go dashing out into the street when he thought of a more interesting engagement.

"He's smart, and he remembers everything, and I could teach him to be the best brewmaster in five counties, but he can't be relied on," said Dirk's father, who ran the local tavern. "He doesn't seem to have a sense of time or urgency."

Indeed, Fiona could have told any of these potential masters that Reed's sense of time and urgency were both dictated by adventurous possibilities: *You must come to the forest with me this minute, to see the moonflowers opening up. . . . The fish will only bite at dawn—wake up now! . . . Fiona, why are you so slow? The fireflies are just coming out.* Tasks that could keep, skills that could be learned over a period of time, those were not things that would hold Reed's interest for long.

"I don't think he'll be a brewer or a carpenter or a blacksmith or a farmer or anything you've envisioned," Thomas told Damiana at the beginning of the summer. Fiona was supposed to be making dinner, but instead was eavesdropping on the conversation as they sat in the main room and sipped tea. His arrival had come as a surprise to Fiona, though Damiana had greeted him as if they had planned this visit a long time ago.

Damiana laughed a little. "Then what will he be? Where will he go?"

"Have you ever thought he might want to seek his father? Go to Wodenderry and try his fortune?"

"No," Damiana said, and her voice was troubled.

"I am sure it has crossed his mind. It's a very lively mind he has, and everything crosses it at some time or another."

Fiona could attest to that. She could also have corroborated Thomas's speculation. Reed *had* talked about going to the royal city to see what he could learn about King Marcus—but he'd also talked about going to Lowford and Thrush Hollow, or moving to Stilton and learning to sail a boat, or bundling up all his belongings in a bag and walking across the entire world. It was hard to know what might seriously catch his fancy.

"Well, we'll see if he likes the merchant life," Damiana said. "And after that—well, we'll just see."

Fiona supposed that meant Damiana might next decide to apprentice Reed to one of the merchants in town—but, it turned out, she supposed wrong. Over dinner that night, their mother laid out an entirely different plan.

"I'd like you both to go spend the summer in Lowford with Angeline," Damiana said. "Reed, I've arranged for you to spend a few months working with Robert Bayliss in his trading business. He's looking forward to teaching you what he knows and I'd like you to be a great help to him if you can. Fiona, Angeline's neighbor Kate is an herbalist like Elminstra, but she cultivates a variety of plants there in the wetter region that Elminstra can't grow here. I think you'll both learn a great deal."

"Marvelous! When do we go?" Reed demanded, but Fiona just stared at her mother.

"But—leave you alone all summer—we can't do that," she said.

Damiana smiled and touched her arm. "I have some projects I'd like to get done around the house, and I won't mind at all being alone. Besides, you know there's never anything like true solitude in a Safe-Keeper's house. And if I get too lonely, I'll walk down to Elminstra's. Or she'll loan me one of her granddaughters to keep me company."

"*I'll* keep you company," Fiona said. "Reed can go this year and I'll go next year."

"Oh, I think it will be much less disruptive to everybody if you both go," Damiana said, her gaze flicking from Fiona to Reed and back again. "Your aunt isn't used to having someone in the house who's as high-spirited as Reed. You can help her . . . contain him."

Reed burst out laughing, and Fiona managed a little smile. It was true that Fiona was the only one who was ever able to instill a sense of direction or purpose in her brother, and he would always do what she asked, even if he didn't like the task. Fiona might be able to keep him more focused on his merchant apprenticeship than either Robert Bayliss or Angeline. Perhaps this whole trip had been planned for Reed's benefit, and Fiona's true role was to help him along. In which case she could not really protest.

"But I hate the idea of leaving you," she said.

"And I'll miss you," Damiana said. "But think what fun you'll have! Angeline is so excited about having you to herself for a whole summer. I'll get a lot done here and be happy to see you when you get back."

"When do we go?" Reed asked again.

"As soon as you can pack," Thomas said. "Tomorrow or the day after."

90

"Tomorrow!" Fiona exclaimed, staring at her mother again.

"I can pack in five minutes," Reed said.

"Or the day after," Damiana amended. "You might need that much time to get used to the idea."

But Fiona still wasn't quite used to the idea when, two days later, they loaded up Thomas's wagon and headed west to Lowford. Damiana had hugged all three of them good-bye and stood at the gate waving gaily as they departed, but Fiona couldn't feel excited about the adventure. Well, she didn't much like adventure anyway. She was always willing to participate in one of Reed's escapades, but those were harmless and close to home. She had never traveled to Lowford—or anywhere—without her mother, and she had to scowl fiercely to keep herself from crying.

The trip itself was monotonous, and Fiona's sadness eventually gave way to boredom. They stopped three or four times to eat and stretch their bones, and pulled into Lowford a little after the noon hour. Angeline lived on the north side of town, on the outskirts like Damiana, so Thomas pointed out various sights as they traveled through the pretty city center. Fiona and Reed had been here before, of course, but not for a couple of years. Fiona had to admit, the bustle of the marketplace and the unfamiliarity of the street arrangements were rather exciting. Lowford was nearly twice as big as Tambleham and a crossroads as well; there was much more going on here than in her own sleepy town.

Angeline was waiting for them at the front door, and hugged them and kissed them as if it had been years since she'd seen them, instead of two months. One arm around Fiona and one around Reed, she looked up at Thomas with a smile. "Are you staying for dinner? There's plenty."

He smiled back. "I think Fiona at least is tired of my company," he said. "But I'll be by from time to time to check on them and take reports back to Tambleham."

"Good," Angeline said. "You're welcome any time."

"Rare words for a Truth-Teller," he commented, and they both laughed.

"Good-bye, then," she said. "Now, my magnificent niece and my adorable nephew, come inside and have dinner. See how happy I am to have you for a whole summer!"

Despite the fact that she missed her mother a great deal, Fiona really did have a wonderful summer. Angeline's friend Kate was thin, tall, fey, and fierce, one of the oddest people Fiona had ever met, but she knew plants like nobody else Fiona had ever encountered. They would wander through Kate's garden completely at random, and the older woman would point to this flower or that herb and rattle off a description of its properties and how it could best be used to cure fever or heartache. They spent hours in her greenhouse, something that Fiona had never seen before. It was constructed carefully of glass and metal and designed to create an indoor climate that was more favorable to certain species than the outdoor one. Inside its transparent walls they would discuss soil, fertilizer, and pests. The entire house appeared to have been given over to cuttings, and everywhere stems and tubers sat in glass jars full of water, sprouting coiled, needle-thin roots. Even the kitchen table, even the kitchen stove, had to be cleared now and then so Kate and Fiona could make or consume a meal.

Kate's visitors were many and various, and they all treated the tall woman as if she were a visionary who might at any moment start speaking in an unintelligible tongue. But Fiona felt right at home with her in a matter of days. There was no subterfuge with Kate, no hidden meaning behind her plain words. She might not speak concisely or always to the point, but she never wasted time on subjects that did not matter. And Fiona learned more than she had ever thought possible.

Reed appeared to be enjoying his summer as well, though he might not have been learning as much. Every day when they returned for dinner, Angeline would quiz them on what they'd discovered that day and how they might incorporate those lessons into their daily lives. Fiona could answer easily, tossing off the names of new plants and the ingredients for new potions, but Reed would often merely shrug and attack his food.

"It was just more logging of entries," he would say. "Nothing new." Or, "We walked around the warehouse and looked at the bins. Can I have more potatoes?" Or, "Did you know Robert owns fifty horses and twenty wagons? *Fifty horses!* The ostlers along the southern route keep stable stalls just for him."

But if asked, he would say he was having a splendid time and that the merchant life might be the one for him after all. Fiona doubted it, but she was glad to hear that he was at least paying attention and managing to do more than simply be a distraction to the other workers while he was supposed to be working.

Robert Bayliss, in fact, seemed to have taken to Reed with all the fondness of an indulgent uncle. "I do enjoy that boy," he told Angeline and Fiona one night over dinner. Angeline had invited both Robert and his wife, Victoria, to join them for the evening meal, and Thomas had arrived unexpectedly. It was quite a convivial gathering, for Thomas had brought letters from Damiana and Robert had brought wine. "He's so full of energy. Nothing slows him down, nothing stops him. Give him a problem and he'll tease at it till he solves it."

"Or forgets about it," Fiona said a little dryly.

Reed grinned. "I've been concentrating."

"It's hard to be a young lad and have to sit still all day, learning dull facts about shipping lanes and freighting weights," Robert said with a smile. "I try to give him some variety."

"Today I helped load grain barrels into the wagons," Reed said with great enthusiasm. "They're heavy! And they roll, unless you swing them just right—"

"And nothing ever bores him," Robert said. "And all my managers like him. I can't remember the last apprentice I've had who seemed so promising."

"Better hire him, then," Thomas recommended.

"He's supposed to have another year of school left," Fiona said with a little frown.

"I don't care if I finish school," Reed said.

"Well, your mother does," Angeline said. "So you can talk about your career next summer."

Victoria, who had said very little during dinner, now touched a cloth napkin to her lips. "Angeline, such a lovely meal. You are so accomplished in all the domestic skills," she said in a faint voice. "But I find—I'm a little tired. Could I go sit in a quiet room somewhere for a few moments?"

Robert was instantly on his feet, bending over her and looking concerned. "Would you like to go home? I'll bring around the carriage."

She gave him a wan smile. "Oh, no. I need to collect my strength before I try to make the journey."

Angeline came around the edge of the table. "I'll take you back to my room so you can lie down for a while. Will that be good?"

"Oh, most excellent. Thank you so much. Robert, you sit here and talk with the others. Angeline will see to me."

They were scarcely out the kitchen door before Reed leaped to his feet. "Thomas! I forgot! Come see my new riding wheel. Robert gave it to me and it's the most amazing thing."

With a nod at the other two, Thomas stood up. "Yes, you must display your proficiency to me so I can go home and tell your mother how accomplished you are."

That quickly, the room emptied out, and Fiona was left alone with Robert, to whom she had never said a word in private in her life. "Would you like something else to eat?" she asked, deciding to play the role of hostess in order to make conversation. "Or I could make some tea. There's cake, too, when everybody comes back."

Robert smiled at her. He really seemed like a gentle man, she thought, and most agreeable. She was sorry for him, shackled to such a difficult wife. "Thank you, but I think I'll wait for that cake," he said. "Your aunt is quite

95

the baker. I would grow fat if I lived in her house."

Fiona laughed. "I try to eat normal portions, but Reed just eats and eats and *eats*. Still, you see how tall he is and still so thin. I suppose he can eat as much as he wants to."

"I do hope I can convince your brother to come work for me next summer," the merchant said. "He's brought so much liveliness to the business! And he's such a joy to be around. If I'd had a son, I would have wanted him to be like Reed."

"You don't have any children?"

He shook his head. "No. I always thought—I always wanted—if the Dream-Maker were here right now, I'd tell her, 'Give me children! And, more specifically, give me a son.'" He laughed a little, as if to soften the demand, but Fiona could hear the deep wistfulness in his voice. "But even she can't help me out, I'm afraid."

"So why didn't you have children?" Fiona asked, trying to make her voice sympathetic so the question didn't sound so blunt.

"Oh, my dear, you can see how fragile Victoria is. She would never withstand the rigors of childbirth."

Fiona gentled her voice even more. "Some miscarriages, then?"

"No, no, nothing like that. Just—we made a decision when we first got married that we wouldn't try to have children of our own."

"But if you had always wanted a son, and you knew she was too frail to have children—" Fiona began. She could tell she was being indelicate, but it simply didn't make sense to her that he had married the woman if she couldn't give him what he wanted. Behind Robert, she saw Thomas enter the kitchen so quietly that the merchant didn't even turn around or appear to notice him.

Robert smiled again, but the expression was full of pain. "She was happy and healthy when we were first betrothed. Then there was an accident, and everything changed. But I would not have considered drawing back from my engagement! And I have always loved her very much. I have had a very good life. It is just this one thing I would change about it if I could. I knew when I married her that she could not have children, and I married her still, for love."

Behind Robert, Thomas opened his mouth. His expression was so cynical that Fiona could almost guess what he planned to say: *Your wife could have children if she so chose. You have let her delude you all these years.* Fiona kept her gaze on Thomas, her face neutral but her eyes full of warning. He smiled a little, turned his head away, and said nothing.

"I think you're a man who is not so very old," Fiona said in a kind voice. "Someday the world may change, and you will find yourself a father after all."

Robert smiled again. "But I cannot wish for the changes that would make such a thing possible. Which is why I need Isadora! To give me all the wishes of my heart at once."

"That is why we all need Isadora," Thomas said, stepping forward then to join the conversation. "Because our hearts are filled with so many wishes."

"I only have one or two," Fiona said.

Thomas took his seat again and studied her. "Given time," he said, "you will think of more."

Reed came knocking through the door again. "Robert!

You didn't come out and see me on the riding wheel! I've gotten so much better."

Robert came instantly to his feet. "Well, then, I'll come watch you for a moment or two." He smiled down at Fiona. "You won't let your aunt serve cake without me, will you?"

"We won't even cut it till you're back," she promised.

He followed Reed out the door, and now she was left face-to-face with Thomas, to whom she had even less to say. "I could make you some tea, if you like," she offered without much enthusiasm.

He grinned. "I could make it myself if I wanted it," he said, stretching out his long legs. "You don't have to wait on me."

She shrugged and made no more effort at conversation.

"So, are you enjoying your summer with Angeline?" he asked.

"Yes, and the days I spend with Kate. I've learned so much, I think I could be the village witch if I wanted."

He tilted his head to one side, studying her with his dark eyes. "Maybe," he said in a musing voice. "But I don't see that as the truth of your future."

"But then, you've never seen the—the 'truth of my future' with any great skill," she said.

He grinned again. "I still say you'll never be a Safe-Keeper."

"I still say you're wrong."

He reached out a hand to toy with a knife left on the table after dinner. "You don't care much for silence. Your passion for justice is too strong. I do not believe you'd be able to keep a desperate secret. You would be much more likely to try and right the wrong."

"You say it as if that would be a flaw on my part."

He spread his hands, the knife glinting in the candle-light. "A flaw in a Safe-Keeper, yes. A flaw in an ordinary human being? Hardly."

"I admit there are things my mother knows that trouble me. But perhaps if they had been whispered to me in confidence, I would understand them better."

"Tell me," he said. "If you weren't going to be a Safe-Keeper, what would you choose to be?"

She was taken aback. No one had ever asked her that. "I would—I would be—"

"And you can't be the village witch, either. It's much the same thing. Elminstra knows at least half of your mother's secrets, and not because your mother repeated them."

"I would go to Wodenderry and sew for the queen," she said at random, laughing a little. "I would learn to train horses to perform in traveling shows. I would sail a boat across the Cormeon Sea and trade for riches in foreign lands."

"You could do any of those things," he said. "Who knows? And you might."

She shook her head. "Not me. I was meant to stay close to the place I was born. The real one who wants assorted adventures is my brother."

"He's not your brother," Thomas said in a silky-soft voice.

Fiona stared at him. "He's—what?"

"He's not your brother."

It was amazing to her how much she hated him at that moment. "He's not my brother by *blood*, but he's my brother in spirit. We were raised together. We protect each other.

99

We believe the same things. He's my soul mate."

Thomas nodded. "That, yes. But he's not your brother. And a time may come when you're glad of it."

She came quickly to her feet. "I can't think of a single time when I've been glad of a thing you said," she told him. She strode from the room and through the kitchen door to the back yard where Reed was demonstrating his talent on the wheel. It was a big spoked circle surmounted by a small seat and propelled by pedals, and Reed was following a wobbly path down the rich summer grass.

"See? I can stay balanced for almost ten minutes now," he was calling. He spotted Fiona. "Look! Can you see how much better I am than I was yesterday?"

"Wonderful," she called. "Can you go faster?"

Of course he could not resist the challenge, and of course he tumbled over almost immediately. Robert cried out in alarm, but Fiona was laughing. Reed, when he scrambled to his feet, was laughing, too.

"Tomorrow I'll go faster," he said. "Robert, I can't tell you how much I love the riding wheel. It's the best present anyone has ever given me."

"Well, you're the best worker I've ever had," the older man said.

Angeline poked her head out the door. "Doesn't anyone want cake? It's chocolate and I'm ready to serve it now."

"She made chocolate for me because it's my favorite," Reed told Robert as they all immediately turned back for the house.

"Maybe she made it for me. It's *my* favorite," Robert replied.

"It's everybody's favorite," Fiona said, slipping inside ahead of both of them. "You're not so special."

They ate quite merrily, all of them—or at least Fiona—managing to forget there was an invalid in the house. But as soon as Robert had finished his piece, he laid down his fork and stood up.

"Time for me to get Victoria home," he said. "It's been a long day for her. Angeline, as always, you have been the most gracious hostess. I have so much enjoyed this evening with you and your charming guests."

Angeline offered to help him guide Victoria to the coach, and Thomas offered to hold the horses, so Reed and Fiona were left to clean up the dishes and sneak another piece of cake. Reed was in an exuberant mood, and as he worked, he talked almost nonstop about Robert and the job and the riding wheel and Thomas and how much he was enjoying this summer in Lowford. Fiona listened and nodded and agreed with all of it except the praise offered to Thomas, though she didn't bother telling Reed how much she disliked the Truth-Teller. It was her own secret, after all, and despite what anyone else might think, she was good at keeping things to herself.

Chapter Eight

ater in the season, about a week before Fiona and Reed were planning to return home, Isadora and Thomas both passed through Lowford at the same time. Angeline had another dinner party, for just the five of them, though it seemed very strange to Fiona that this particular group of people would gather together without her mother also being present. She supposed Isadora and Thomas often visited Angeline when they came to Lowford, and that seemed wrong, too. It was hard to believe that people could have lives and associations that went on when Fiona and Reed and Damiana were not there to witness them and participate.

Isadora, it turned out, hadn't been to Tambleham all summer. "So I have no news for you," she said. "But isn't it about time for you two to be going home?"

"Next week," Fiona and Reed said in unison. She was happy about it; he was not. It was not that he didn't want to see his mother and his friends again; he just hated to leave behind the new friends and new pastimes he had discovered in Lowford.

Isadora glanced at Thomas. "Are you escorting them back?"

He shook his head.

"I am," Angeline said rather quickly. "I want to visit my sister for a while."

Isadora nodded. "Well, I'll be by before Wintermoon if I can. But certainly I'll be there for the holiday."

"Where have your travels taken you recently?" Angeline asked.

Isadora looked sorrowful for a moment. "Oh, I was just at my daughter's in Thrush Hollow for the week. Her husband has fallen sick with a lung ailment. That poor girl, she's had so much suffering in her life, I think she must be destined to be Dream-Maker after me. Though I don't say that to her face, of course. She tries hard not to blame me for all her troubles, but sometimes I think—well, I won't be going back there for a while. It might be easier on all of us."

"Tell us somewhere else you've been," Reed said. "A place where happier things occurred."

They all smiled a little at that. "Well, of course you've heard the splendid news," Isadora said. "I was in the royal city about ten months ago and just this week the young queen had a baby boy! You can imagine the celebration they're planning."

"Unfortunately, the baby is not the king's," Thomas said coolly.

Angeline and Isadora exclaimed aloud at this. Fiona merely looked at him with narrowed eyes. "You can't be

103

serious!" Angeline said. "Surely the queen wouldn't—I mean, every eye is upon her—"

"But are you *sure?*" Isadora said. "Everyone says that she seems so happy."

Thomas shrugged. "I tell the truth as it makes itself known to me—and I doubt I'm the only Truth-Teller to know this fact. There may be a Safe-Keeper or two who's been told this secret, but I believe this is one truth that will wriggle out, and fairly soon."

"Oh, dear. Well, that's a true shame," Isadora said. "I hope I wasn't helping to grant anybody's wishes in this case— oh, dear—"

"Well, I don't think this is very happy news either," Reed said. "Don't you have any stories that have better endings?"

"Let's see . . . in Marring Cross a young man proposed to the girl he loved and she accepted him. That was a happy ending," Isadora said. "But I think true love prevails even without the services of the Dream-Maker."

"Or this world would be an even sadder place than it is," Angeline agreed, coming to her feet. "Would anyone like dessert? Fiona and I made a cherry tart this afternoon."

"Now that's *my* dream come true," Reed said. Everyone laughed.

After that they made tea and ate sweets and talked late into the night. Both guests were gone by morning, after promising to meet again no later than Wintermoon. Fiona spent her final week in Kate's garden, taking prized cuttings and listening intently to the detailed instructions on how to care for them.

In a week, Fiona and Reed and Angeline were packing their belongings and piling into a comfortable traveling carriage that Robert had insisted on lending them. Fiona and Reed leaned out the windows to watch the town fold back behind them, but Angeline merely sat with her head resting against the back of the seat, and looked as if she was tired before the journey had even begun.

When they were not far from the outskirts of Tambleham, only about two miles from their own house, the carriage came to a complete halt. "*Now* what?" Angeline exclaimed, because they'd been stopped twice already on the road, once by a flooded river and once by a felled tree.

Reed craned his head out the window. "It looks like—it looks like a hay cart has dropped its load all over the road," he said. "Oh! And there's another wagon. I think maybe they collided and the hay got knocked out. The horses are sideways across the road, too."

Angeline looked alarmed. "Is anyone hurt?"

"Not that I can see. They all look mad, though."

"Can we drive around?" Fiona asked.

"Field's pretty wet," Reed observed. "Might get stuck."

"I don't think I can bear to sit one more hour on the road," Angeline said.

Reed had already pulled the handle and opened his door. "I'm going to walk the last couple of miles," he said. "I'll be home before you."

He had one foot out the door when Angeline said, "Wait."

He turned back with an inquiring look on his face. Fiona

105

was already staring at her aunt. Angeline had been so quiet during the whole long journey that Fiona had assumed she was sleepy, or maybe had developed a headache from the rock and clatter of the coach. But now something in Angeline's taut features and expression of misery gave Fiona a creeping, bone-deep chill.

"What is it?" Fiona asked in a low voice. "What's wrong?"

"There is—when you get home—you'll find that your mother's been sick," Angeline said.

Reed drew his foot back in and shut the door very carefully. Fiona said, "How sick?"

Angeline shook her head. "I don't know. We both thought—and even Elminstra thought—if she spent the summer very quietly, doing nothing, she might recover. That's why you both came to stay with me. And Elminstra went to see her every day, and tried every potion she knew. But she—but your mother—she hasn't gotten stronger. She's gotten weaker instead."

"How weak?" Fiona asked in the same clipped voice.

"I don't know. I haven't seen her. But Thomas says she's very frail."

Without another word, Reed palmed the handle, shoved open the door, and jumped out of the coach. Fiona called after him, but he was already ten yards away, racing at a full-out run across the fields, by the shortest route back to the cottage.

Fiona returned her attention to her aunt. She was furious. "How could you do this?" she whispered. "How could you take us away from her when there might not be very much time left?"

Angeline shook her head. "Our hope was to make her better, not to keep you away from her."

"How could you not tell us such an important thing?"

"She asked me not to," Angeline said starkly. "And I'm a Safe-Keeper."

"And Thomas? He knew?"

"He knew."

"And *he* did not tell me? *He*, who repeats every thought the minute it pops into his head? He knew, and he didn't tell me?"

"Sometimes," Angeline said sadly, "a Truth-Teller can choose not to speak. It is just that nothing he says is false."

"I hate you both," Fiona said flatly, and got out of the coach.

She could not run as fast as Reed, but she was a good walker, and she knew the way as well as Reed did. The ground was muddy but only impassable in a few spots, and she followed Reed's footprints around any particularly marshy places. She was so full of rage and fear that she almost was not aware of her feet moving and her body working. Her skin was hot from sun or exertion or terror, but her heart was cold.

No one had had to speak the truth out loud for Fiona to know that her mother was dying.

She was panting a little by the time she made it in sight of the cottage. The garden looked overgrown, as if no one had tended it all season. The back door was open, as if Reed had run through without bothering to close it behind him. The carriage with Angeline was nowhere in sight—it was probably still stuck behind the hay cart two miles down the road.

Fiona pushed herself to a run and hurried through the back door, into the welcome coolness of the cottage. Damiana and Reed were right there inside the kitchen. He was on his knees and weeping into her skirt; she was standing there gazing down at him, her arms cradled around his head.

She looked up and smiled when Fiona burst in. "I hope you were not cruel to Angeline," she said, and her voice was raspy, as if she had been crying or coughing or simply not talking very much. "None of this is her fault."

It was Reed who had always been able to express whatever the emotion of the day brought; Fiona was not able to fall to her knees and lament, much as she wanted to. She merely stared at her mother and read the story in her eyes.

"This was a secret you could have trusted me with," she said.

Damiana shook her head. "This was a secret I never wanted to tell," she replied.

Angeline did not come to the door for several more hours, though Fiona thought she heard the coach lumber by the front gate about a half hour later. By that time, Reed had calmed down enough to sit and have tea, and the three of them were gathered together at the kitchen table, talking.

"How much time?" Reed asked.

Damiana shook her head. "I'm not sure."

"Till Wintermoon?"

"Maybe not."

"I'm not going back to school," he said.

"Of course you are! You—"

"I'm not, either," Fiona said.

Damiana looked at her helplessly, as if she had been counting on Fiona's support. "But I want you to finish your studies. Both of you."

Fiona shrugged and sipped her tea. "I don't think there's anything you can make us do right now. Except take care of you."

"That is not what I would choose for you," Damiana said softly. "Spending precious months of your life tending a dying woman."

"You have already taken away three of those precious months," Fiona said, her voice unyielding. "We're making sure we have the rest."

Reed looked over at Fiona. His happy, carefree face was set and serious; he looked like a different person. "I can keep the garden and do whatever has to be done around the house," he said. "And I'm better at math than you are, so I'll buy the goods we need in town."

"We might need money," Fiona answered him. Both of them ignored Damiana's small wordless exclamations of distress. "I can see if Lacey has any piecework I can do here at the house."

"Dirk might let me work at the tavern a day or two a week. He's asked me before."

"Fiona, Reed—don't talk that way—"

"And I have some cuttings I brought back from Kate's garden," Fiona said, still speaking only to her brother. "Some things that Elminstra doesn't have. I can make some potions up, see if they make things easier for Mother."

"Fiona, darling, don't pin your hopes on your herbal remedies," Damiana murmured.

"One's for pain," Fiona added, as if Damiana hadn't spoken. "In case nothing else works. It's gotten a good solid rooting, too. I can probably pick a few of the leaves tomorrow."

"Don't talk like this," Damiana implored.

Fiona looked over at her mother, at her hurt, hopeful face, seeing the first faint ravages of the disease and the thin lines traced by fear. "We will take care of you," she said in a precise voice. "All you have left to do now is realize how much we love you."

Angeline arrived at dinnertime, in company with Elminstra, who brought a casserole. The old witch came rushing in, throwing her arms around Reed and Fiona in turn, whether they wished to be hugged or not. Fiona felt some of her hardheld anger and panic melt a little against Elminstra's comforting embrace. She took a deep gulping breath and had to fight hard not to start crying into the freshly starched linen of the older woman's dress.

But she controlled herself and stepped away. "Thank you so much for all you've done for my mother while we've been gone," she said.

"Yes, and I was glad to do it, and I'd do it another three

months or another three years," Elminstra exclaimed. "But it is good to see you back, you and your brother—she has missed you so terribly—"

"Elminstra has brought us dinner," Angeline said in a subdued voice. "And will stay to eat it with us if we'd like."

"Yes, please stay," said Reed, and that settled it. Fiona laid another place and they all sat down together and ate.

The meal was the strangest one Fiona could ever remember. Damiana and Elminstra asked hundreds of questions about how their summer had gone, what they had learned from Robert, from Kate, what marvels they had seen in Lowford. Elminstra in turn related bits of gossip, news of events that had transpired over the summer and that might not have made their way into their mother's letters. Reed talked easily, though without his usual buoyancy, but both Fiona and Angeline were quiet, monosyllabic when they spoke at all.

And yet, for all the awkwardness, it was an infinitely precious meal, one that Fiona would never forget, for here they were all together in one room, the four people she loved the most in the world. Someday soon to be reduced to three.

Someday after that—maybe not so far distant a day—to be reduced again, when Elminstra died, or Angeline. It had not occurred to Fiona till this very moment, but that was the normal run of things; adults passed on, children became adults, more children were born. What she had now, this circle of beloved faces, might come together again only a few more times in her life, and who knew when the next member might be culled? Panic gripped her so tightly that her hand shook on her water glass and she had to set it back on the table unsipped.

"Fiona," Damiana said in a quiet voice. "I want you to take your aunt out to the garden and show her the fleurmint you planted this spring. It bloomed for the first time yesterday, and she's never seen it."

Fiona nodded blindly and pushed her chair back. She did not even look over at Angeline, but stepped away from the table and out the back door before anyone else could say a word. Outside, it was dark already, the early dark of late summer, and the smells of laden orchards and cut hay were very strong. In the faint moonlight, Fiona could see only high shadows where the tall stalks of hollyhocks should be, and a low furze of darkness where the summer vegetables lay in their cradles of green.

Angeline stepped outside, the door knocking shut behind her, and Fiona whirled around. It was as if the sobs were breaking her from the inside, snapping her in two bone by bone. Angeline said nothing, merely took Fiona in her arms and held her as long as the crying lasted.

Chapter Nine

What Fiona remembered about the rest of that season was Reed's gentleness. The boy whose chatter could only be stilled by sleep, the boy who ran so fast he could only be caught by nightfall, became a young man who could sit still and silent for hours at a time. It was Reed who brought Damiana her breakfast in the morning, and Reed who carried her from room to room when she grew too weak to walk. It was Reed who sat and read to her for hours, or listened when she had the strength to talk. He did the household chores he had promised—weeded the garden, chopped the wood, shopped in the market, fixed the gate—but more of his time was spent indoors than out, his hand always on their mother's arm.

Fiona, who would have said that she was the one better suited to caretaking, found that she could not bear the quiet vigils for long. She busied herself in the kitchen, cooking and canning; she made daily treks to Elminstra's to fetch more serums or a new soothing tea that the witch thought might ease Damiana's coughing. She tried making her own potions against pain, using cuttings brought back from Kate's garden, and stirred these into her mother's juice every morning. She greeted visitors at the door, and admitted them when she thought they might lift her mother's spirits, and turned them away when she was sure they would not. She would have sent them all away, every one—how dare they intrude on these last few weeks when there was so little time left—except that she could tell Damiana was renewed by the visits, made happy by the small attentions. But she watched in some jealousy as friends from the village sat and laughed with her mother, making her forget, however briefly, that she was sick, that she was dying. Fiona herself did not have that gift. She had love, and she had grief, and she had strength, but she did not have the ability to pretend.

At the end of every day, Reed would carry Damiana to her room, and Fiona would go in to ask if she needed anything else and talk over the day, as Damiana had always done with her. At these times, Fiona tried her best to speak lightly, to gossip about the villagers, and laugh when the subject seemed appropriate; she would see Damiana's face lighten, and she knew exactly what her mother was thinking. *Fiona will survive this after all. She will be strong enough to continue when I am gone.* And every night, she tried to leave the room while her mother still had that look of hope on her face, and every night she would return to the main room and weep.

And every night Reed would come and sit beside her and put his arm around her waist and hold her until the tears stopped. "How can you be so strong?" she whispered to him one night, when she did not think she would ever be able to stop crying.

"It's the only thing I know how to do," he said. "To take care of her, and take care of you."

She wept even harder. "You should not have to take care of me, too! I at least should not be a burden."

He kissed her on the top of her head. "No burden," he murmured. "Love never is."

Damiana was well enough to celebrate their birthday, which fell at the very end of summer or the very beginning of autumn, depending on how you calculated. She had slept most of the day, so she was almost lively at dinnertime when Reed carried her into the main room. Elminstra and one of her daughters and two of her grandchildren came with presents and a chocolate cake, and they had a very festive time of it. The event exhausted Damiana, though, and she slept straight through till noon the next day.

Thomas arrived about six weeks later. By this time, it was near the end, and Damiana was truly dying; death no longer kept any secrets from her. She had finally asked them to send for her sister, who had promised to come stay in the final days. Angeline had visited every week or two, but Fiona and Reed had always assured her they were managing just fine, they did not need any help, the situation was not desperate yet. And so she had gone back home, and Fiona and Reed had had another week with their mother, and another.

But she had grown so weak in the past few days that she

could not move from her bedroom. Reed no longer carried her to the kitchen to take her meals, or out to the main room so she could watch the fire dancing on the hearth. He stayed and talked to her whenever she was awake; when she slept, he went outside and attacked with fierce energy whatever chore he had set himself for the day.

Fiona had sent for Angeline the day before and here she was, arriving with the Truth-Teller in tow.

"How is she?" Angeline demanded, tripping out of his wagon.

"Worse," Fiona said. She was looking up at Thomas, a little frown on her face.

Angeline brushed past her without another word. Fiona still gazed up at Thomas. "I haven't seen her in two months," he said, still sitting on the wagon seat with the reins in his hands. "I gave you that much time."

"Are you going to stay?" she asked.

"It's up to you."

"Up to my mother, you mean."

He shook his head. "Your decision. You're the one who doesn't like me. I wouldn't want to trouble your last days with her."

Fiona felt her shoulders sag. "She was asking about you just yesterday," she said, turning away from him. "It will do her good to see you. You can stay as long as you like."

He did not move, either to step down from the wagon or urge his horses forward so he could stable them in town. "Till the end?" he asked.

"Yes," she answered, and walked on into the house without another glance in his direction.

116

Soon enough, they were all in the house together, Angeline in visiting with her sister, Fiona making the evening meal, Thomas and Reed in the main room talking before the fire. All they were missing was Isadora for it to be like Wintermoon.

Not at all like Wintermoon.

Damiana slept through the meal, so the four of them ate around the kitchen table, conversing quietly, catching up. First there was local news to tell, of Kate in Lowford and Lacey in Tambleham, and then their attention wandered to broader topics.

"Did you hear about the scandal in Wodenderry?" Angeline asked, shaking her head.

"No," Fiona replied. She rarely bothered listening anymore when people talked of anything but illness and remedies. "What happened?"

"The queen and her baby son have fled the city!"

Fiona glanced at Thomas. "So you were right, then."

He nodded. "I was not the brave Truth-Teller who informed the king that the baby was not his, but some reckless woman stepped forward and said that very thing. He had her taken into custody, to be tried for treason, but three more Truth-Tellers rushed to her defense and told the same tale."

"So the king sent for the queen, to ask her for the truth in a public hearing, but she was already gone," Angeline supplied. "*And* one of the king's guards with her. Thereby more or less proving the truth of the accusations."

"What happened to that woman? The one the king imprisoned?" Fiona asked.

117

Thomas gave her a little smile, as if the question did her credit. "Released that day and given a gold ring by way of apology. Though I still don't think the king will be welcoming Truth-Tellers to his palace any time soon."

"Does that mean Princess Lirabel will be named his heir after all?" Reed asked.

Thomas spread his hands. "King Marcus seems to be a most determined man. He may already be looking for a new queen."

Angeline put her hands to her heart as if to stop its mad fluttering. "Time for me to head for the royal city and try to catch the eye of the king!"

"He might be looking for someone a little younger," Thomas observed.

Angeline laughed. "Then I won't waste my time."

"I'd like to see the royal city someday," Reed said.

"And you should," Thomas said. "It's a beautiful, wicked, holy, crowded, fascinating, and wonderful place." He glanced at Fiona. "You should both go sometime."

Fiona shook her head. "I'd rather stay right here."

The next few days passed quite quietly, considering how many people were in the house. Thomas and Reed were mostly outside, doing heavy repairs to the shed out back and reframing one of the windows on the upper story of the house. Angeline took over Reed's job of sitting with Damiana most of the day. Fiona, who continued her tasks of cooking and cleaning, could occasionally hear their voices as she passed the doorway to her mother's room. Often, it was

Angeline talking, telling light, meaningless stories designed to make Damiana smile; but sometimes Damiana was the one speaking, her voice very faint and low. Fiona did not need to ask what Damiana was telling her sister. She was passing on the secrets that needed to be kept, that someone must know even though the Safe-Keeper was gone. Angeline listened gravely, and nodded, and added the words to her own stores of secret knowledge.

One afternoon while Fiona was rolling out a pastry crust to make a meat pie for dinner, Angeline came from the sickroom. "Your mother would like a glass of water," she said. "And she'd like you to take it to her."

Fiona looked up, inquiring. "Is she feeling worse?"

Angeline shrugged. "Well enough to talk for a while. I think there are things she wants to tell you."

Fiona did her best to brush the flour from her hands. "All right. Can you finish this?"

A few minutes later she carried the water into her mother's room. Damiana was sitting up in bed, looking pale but determined. Her dark hair was pulled back into a braid and her skin looked white and exposed. Her eyes were dark and hollowed, just now glittering with a hint of fever. But she smiled when Fiona came in.

"Something smells good," Damiana said. "You must be making dinner."

"Meat pie," Fiona said, handing her the glass and sitting on one of the two chairs pulled up next to the bed. "Elminstra's recipe. Maybe you'll be hungry enough to eat some later."

"I might just be," Damiana agreed. "You've turned into such a good cook. And gardener. I'm amazed at everything you know and do."

Fiona smiled. "Be more amazed at Reed and everything he's learned. Who'd have thought it of such a restless boy?"

Damiana sighed. "I wish I knew," she said, "what you will both choose with your lives. That's what I regret most—having to leave before I have seen you both settled."

"I'll be a Safe-Keeper and Reed will be—something different every year," Fiona said. "And we'll both be happy and we'll both think of you every day."

"Even if you don't choose to become a Safe-Keeper," Damiana said slowly, "there is one secret you need to know."

"Something I can never tell?" Fiona asked.

"You'll be able to tell it one day," Damiana said. "And you'll know when." And she leaned forward and whispered the secret in Fiona's ear.

Fiona listened and nodded, and then they both sat back. She tried to keep the expression on her face unchanging, but inside she was amazed and full of churning wonder. "And I can't even tell Reed?" she said.

"Not yet."

"But I'll know when I can?"

"If you don't, Thomas will know."

Now Fiona couldn't keep the displeasure from showing on her face. "Thomas knows this secret?"

Damiana shook her head. "Oh, no. I would not trust him to keep such a thing. But he'll know when it should no longer be a secret."

"Thank you for trusting me," Fiona said formally.

Damiana smiled and reached over to squeeze Fiona's hand. Her grip was pitifully weak. "I would trust you with any secret," she said.

Four days later, Damiana died. It was as if, after sharing all her information with Angeline and Fiona, she had nothing very important left to do, and so she began dozing for longer and longer hours and waking up for shorter and shorter periods of time. Angeline, Reed, and Thomas took turns sitting in the room with her, holding her hand and watching the deepening serenity on her face. Fiona kept busy with the chores of the house, dropping by the sickroom now and then to see if anything was wanted, but not able to bear the idea of staying for longer than a few minutes. She did not understand how the others could wait with such patience for such an unwelcome guest; she did not want to be nearby when Death made his visit.

Elminstra came by twice a day, bringing teas and potions. Every time she left, she was quietly crying. The evening of that fourth day, while Angeline and Thomas sat with Damiana, the witch called Reed and Fiona together.

"It will be tonight," she told them, her voice calm even though tears rolled down her smooth cheeks. "Say your good-byes to her, make it plain to her that you let her go. Or she may try to linger another day or two, and there's no purpose to that."

"Is she still awake?" Fiona asked. "Can she understand us?"

Elminstra made an equivocal gesture with one hand.

"Not really awake, not really sleeping. Can she hear you? I don't know. But I firmly believe she can sense you, can catch the echoes of your emotions. And she will know if you're not ready to let her go."

Fiona looked to one side. "I'm not," she said.

Reed put his arm around her. He was so tall now that she felt tiny next to him, a kitten protected by a playful but occasionally ferocious kitchen dog. "Yes, you are," he said, and his voice was comforting. "We both are. You can do this."

She looked up at him. "You'll have to do it," she said.

The two of them ate dinner alone together, saying very little, then Fiona fixed plates for Angeline and Thomas. Hand in hand, she and Reed slowly walked to Damiana's room.

"We'll sit with her a while," Reed announced. "You two go eat."

Angeline stood up, her face apprehensive. Thomas rose to his feet more slowly. "Did she—what did Elminstra say when she left?" Angeline asked.

"She told us to make our good-byes," Reed said gently.

A little sob escaped Angeline. Thomas nodded at them, his shadowed face looking stark with grief. "We have already done so," he said, and wheeled and left the room. Angeline, crying silently, followed behind him.

Reed pushed Fiona forward and they took their places in the two chairs positioned beside the bed. Fiona took her mother's hand, since she was sitting closest to where the thin fingers lay, and Reed reached up to brush the dark hair from Damiana's forehead. He nodded at Fiona, as if she must be the one to speak first.

"Elminstra told us—Elminstra said it was time to say—say good-bye," Fiona said, her voice faltering. "You have taught us—everything you can—and we are grateful for all that. Every word. Every whisper. Every secret." She tried to say more but the words wouldn't come. She looked over at Reed and shook her head. Her eyes burned and her chest was tight, but not a single tear would gather and fall.

Damiana stirred just a little. Fiona could feel the stick-like fingers tighten on her own, and her mother's lips gathered as if she would speak, but no sound came.

"Ssshh," Reed whispered, leaning over to kiss her on the forehead, on the closed eyelids. "No words now. Nothing more to tell. Time for you to rest now." He kissed her again, forehead, cheek. "Magical sleeping kisses. Here's another one. You'll rest now, with no dreaming. Another magical sleeping kiss, and another—"

It took only a few more kisses before Damiana sighed and relaxed. Fiona felt the clenched fingers uncurl, saw the calm expression come to her mother's face. With a smothered cry, she struggled to her feet and blundered through the door. Angeline caught her before she had gone three steps down the hall.

Part

Chapter Ten

It was clear that it had never occurred to Angeline that there would be any resistance to her plan. "But of course you're both coming back with me to Lowford," she said blankly over breakfast three days later. The funeral was over, Thomas was gone, and the house was a still, sad place. "You can't stay here by yourselves."

"I'm not leaving Tambleham," Fiona said quietly. She was too tired to argue or even be particularly polite. "Reed can go if he likes."

Just moments ago, Reed had expressed a willingness to come live with Angeline and continue his apprenticeship with Robert Bayliss, and Fiona's decision had surprised him as much as it had surprised Angeline. "I'm not leaving if you're not," he said.

"Of course you are! You both are!" Angeline exclaimed. "You can't possibly—two sixteen-year-old children living alone—it's unthinkable."

"There's the house and the garden," Fiona said calmly. "They have to be cared for. And someone in town needs to be Safe-Keeper."

"The house can be sold, and Safe-Keepers can be found in villages half a day's ride in any direction," Angeline said firmly. "You're coming back to Lowford with me."

"Actually," said Fiona, "I'm not."

She had worked it all out, and by dinnertime, with Elminstra's help, she had convinced them all. She would stay in the house by day, tending the garden; she would go to Elminstra's in the evenings, so that no one needed to worry about a young unprotected girl sleeping alone at night.

"And, you know, my granddaughter Allison has been planning to come study with me next year," Elminstra said. "She's nearly twenty now. The two of them can live here together and do quite well."

"But still! Two young women alone!" Angeline cried.

Reed shrugged. "Fiona's pretty good at handling things. And Elminstra is just down the road."

"So you see I'll be just fine," Fiona said. "I won't be alone and I'm not afraid."

"It still seems wrong," Angeline said, but it was clear her arguments were exhausted. "Any time you change your mind, of course, you just catch the fastest coach heading west. I'll always have a room waiting for you."

"I'll be back all the time," Reed said. "You won't have a chance to miss me."

Fiona looked at him with a little smile. "You," she said, "nothing will keep you in Tambleham—or Lowford, either. I'd miss you even if I was going to live there with you and Angeline."

"He'll settle down someday," Elminstra said. "You'll see."

"Well, I'm settled already," Fiona said. "Nobody needs to worry about me."

Thus began Fiona's first year as a Safe-Keeper. The first few weeks were unbelievably quiet and a little lonely, since no one needed the services of a Safe-Keeper and Fiona had rarely spent any time in her mother's cottage by herself. But she found she liked the silence, the chance to operate just exactly as she chose. She might sort through her seeds one day, and spend the next day doing nothing but reading. She took in piecework from Lacey and sewed when she felt like it, and didn't sew when she didn't feel like it. Now that the house was empty, she rarely bothered to cook, just opened and ate from one of the jars of vegetables that she had canned during the fall.

She did some rearranging in the house. Angeline had helped her clear out some of her mother's things, but Fiona redid the room from top to bottom, sewing new curtains and putting down a new rug and moving the bed to the other wall. Then she made this room her own room, and turned her upstairs bedroom into a guest room, with new sheets and curtains of its own.

Reed's room she left exactly as it was.

She cut back an overgrown hedge in the front yard and planned where she would lay in new flowerbeds in the spring. She trimmed the kirrenberry tree, grown quite ragged, and buried a lock of her mother's hair under its soundless shade. On one of his many visits, Reed brought her the roots and half a foot of truelove, so she planted it at the front porch to see if it would take this late in the season. It did, and its heart-shaped leaves were soon sending spiraling tendrils around the lintel of the door. When the first frost came, all the hearts turned red, and soon held drifts of white snow against their vivid skins.

A week before Wintermoon, Fiona had her first customer. It was late afternoon and she was standing at the front gate, checking to make sure that a recalcitrant latch was working better now that it was oiled. She didn't look up at the sound of the approaching wagon until it came to a halt and a passenger alighted. Then she realized that Calbert Seston was holding the reins of the wagon and Megan Henshaw was coming toward the gate to see her.

"Good afternoon," Fiona said, her voice civil and neutral. It was unlikely that this was a purely social call; she encountered these two all the time in the village, and they always said hello, but it wasn't as if either of them would claim to be Fiona's friend. Still, they might want nothing more than a leaf of truelove to add to a Wintermoon wreath. Fiona had already handed out a dozen of them.

"Good afternoon," Megan said in a low voice. The pretty girl had grown into a lovely young woman, but she did not look like a happy one. Her face was puckered from cold, and her expression was anxious. "Could I—do you have time to talk to me?"

"Certainly," Fiona said. "Would you like to step inside?"

"I'll be back in an hour," Calbert called. Megan didn't bother to answer him and he didn't wait for a reply, just set the horses in motion.

"Yes, inside," Megan answered.

"I'll make tea," Fiona said.

They were seated at the table sipping mint tea before Megan spoke again. "You're—I came to see if you could give me a potion," the older girl said. "You cultivate herbs and plants that no one else in this part of the country can grow."

Fiona stirred her tea. "I do, but I don't have everything Elminstra has, and I don't know as many recipes," she said slowly. "You might be better off to go to her."

"I can't ask her this. She's my mother's second cousin. I can't get any potion from her."

Now Fiona looked at her, very direct. "What is it that you want this drug to do?"

The answer was really no surprise. "I want to make sure I don't become pregnant with Cal's baby," she said. "Not now. Not yet. We aren't to be married for at least another year. You must have something that I can take that will— that will keep such a thing from happening. And you must keep it a secret."

Fiona nodded. "I do. I will. But there is also—you know that there is one sure way to not conceive a baby."

Megan gave a wild little laugh. "Oh, but I can't say no to Cal. He is—he is very insistent. He is so used to having his way. It is much easier just to do what he wants."

"Well, I have some herbs I can give you. You have to make sure you take some every day, and never skip a day. But if you do that, you should be protected."

"And you won't tell anyone?"

Fiona shook her head. "I won't tell anyone."

Megan dropped her eyes to her teacup and cradled her hand around its delicate shape. "Cal was so angry with me last night," she said. "I refused him. I had thought, a week ago, that I might be . . . and I did not want to risk it. But he said he would not marry me next year if I would not do what he says now."

"You came to me for potions, not for advice, but let me offer some advice anyway," Fiona said. "Don't marry Cal Seston next year, or ever."

"I have to," Megan said, still whispering. "My father said—"

"Someday your father will be dead, and Cal Seston's father too. And you'll still be alive and married to Cal. Think about that when you're thinking about how much you want to please your father."

Megan looked away again. "But where would I go? What would I do?"

Fiona shrugged. "Where do you want to go? What do you want to do?"

Megan laughed on a soft exhalation of breath. "Go to the royal city and meet the king. I'd marry one of his courtiers and live in the palace and be rich."

Fiona grinned. "Sounds better than marrying Cal Seston."

Now Megan gave a real laugh. "But much less likely!"

"That's what we have dreams for," Fiona said.

They talked a while longer and then Fiona went into the pantry where she kept her dried herbs. She brought out two kinds, one with a harsh taste that was easy on the stomach, one with a sweeter taste that sometimes made the patient sick.

"I prefer the bitter one," Fiona said. "But it is up to you."

"I will try them both, and see what I like best," Megan said, standing up quickly. Outside, they could hear the wagon pulling up before the gate and the sound of Cal's impatient voice raised. "Thank you," Megan said and threw her arms around Fiona's neck. "I can't . . . thank you."

"Come back if I can help you with something else," Fiona said.

She saw her visitor to the door but did not escort her out to the gate. It was getting dark and a little chilly and she did not particularly want to see Cal Seston again.

When she returned to the kitchen, she was to be even more surprised than she had been by Megan's embrace: The other woman had left two gold coins on the table next to her teacup.

Payment for a Safe-Keeper's services.

Isadora was the first to arrive for Wintermoon. "Is it all right that I'm here?" she asked as she climbed down from the carriage and waved good-bye to her benefactors. "As I started to come here, I thought—well, it's all different now. I thought maybe you were all at Angeline's and maybe I should go there, or find somewhere else to go, and I *can*, even at this late date—"

But Fiona was hugging her, pulling her toward the house, laughing as she had not laughed in days. "No, I am *so*

133

glad you're here! Angeline and Reed are arriving tomorrow, but I had no way to get in touch with you—no one ever knows where you are. Oh, it is good to see you!"

They talked late into the night, for this was one evening Fiona would not have to trudge down to Elminstra's to sleep in that crowded house. Isadora was grieved that she hadn't been able to make it to Damiana's funeral, but there had been tragedy in her own life just then, her sister dying after a sudden illness.

"I swear, there are times I don't think I can carry this burden another day, let alone another year," Isadora said with a sigh. "And then I pass through Movington, as I did yesterday, and I discover that the little girl who was so sick last time I was there grew well two days after I left. They had been afraid that she would lose her hearing and they brought her to me. Well, I don't know how to cure a child—I don't know why I have the power in me that I have, or how it works, or why it chooses to grant one wish and not another. But I kissed that little girl on each of her ears and I rocked her for a while and sang a lullaby. And when I passed through yesterday and they spotted me in the coach, we almost could not make it down the street. The whole village mobbed us and called out my name, and cheered when we were finally able to pull free. And I thought, 'Well, perhaps it is worth it after all.'"

"You might be able to help make a dream come true here in Tambleham," Fiona said. "And you won't need any magic to do it."

"Why, how's that?"

"Do you know anyone in the royal city who needs a

young woman for a companion? An old woman, maybe, with connections at the palace. I know a girl here who is bright and pretty and eager to get away. If you had someone to send her to—"

"I can't think of anyone at the moment, but I'm going to Wodenderry after Wintermoon," Isadora said. "I'll inquire and see what I can discover. So you are playing intriguer as well as Safe-Keeper here in your little cottage!"

"And wood witch as well, since people come to me now and then for potions."

"Does Elminstra mind?"

Fiona smiled a bit sardonically. "Most of the ones who come to me for elixirs would not trouble Elminstra with these requests."

"Well, you're young to carry all these burdens," Isadora said. "Don't forget to be a girl yourself while you can."

Fiona shook her head. "That time is past," she said quietly. "And this is who I am now."

Angeline and Reed arrived in the morning, along with the first snowfall of the season. Impossibly, Reed seemed to have grown another inch in the two weeks since Fiona had seen him, and he instantly filled the house with his happy presence. They left the two older women to bake the bread and begin making the sweets, and they spent three hours tramping through the familiar woods, gathering branches.

"And Robert? How's he?"

"Wonderful. You can tell Robert anything and he understands."

Fiona felt a twinge of alarm. "Why, what have you told him?"

"Oh, that I'm not sure I want to spend the winter in Lowford. It's too far from you, for one thing, and I'm tired of the work, for another. It's not that it's too hard, it's just that—I don't know! There are so many other things I haven't done! I haven't been to Merendon to see the great boats, I haven't gone north to the mines to watch them haul out copper. I haven't—I haven't been anywhere, I haven't done anything. I don't want to settle down and be a merchant my whole life until I know for sure that's what I want."

"Well, I don't think you'll be any closer to me if you move to Merendon or the northern cities," Fiona observed.

Reed grinned. "No, but I might stay in Tambleham for the winter, and head down to Merendon in the spring. By then you'll have remembered how quiet the cottage is without me, and you'll be glad to see me go."

"I'd be happy to have you, even for a season," she said seriously. "But I hate to see you leave Robert on bad terms—"

"No, truly, he was as nice as could be. Said I could come back in the fall and work again. Every fall, until I figured out what I wanted to do next. So I said I thought I would."

She shook her head. "How can you be so restless and I so settled?"

"Different fathers," he said with a smile. "Different mothers, too, though we forget that. Not a single drop of blood in our veins that we share."

"Strange," she said, smiling back, "when we share everything else."

Not until the morning of Wintermoon itself did Thomas arrive at the door. No one had asked about him, though Fiona noticed that both Isadora and Angeline lifted their heads to listen every time a wagon seemed to slow down as it went by the house. She knew they thought she had told him to make other plans for the holiday, but they did not want to ask the question outright, preferring to hope that it was not true.

That morning, while they were still at the breakfast table, there finally came the sound that they had all listened for—a wagon coming to a halt at the front gate.

"Is that—I wonder who that could be?" Isadora said.

Fiona stood up. "I'll go see."

But it was, as she had known it would be, the Truth-Teller. He sat in the front of the wagon, the reins wrapped around his hands, waiting for her to step from the house. She pushed through the gate and came to stand right by the wagon, her hand resting on the footrest on the passenger's side.

"We were afraid you weren't coming," she said.

He looked down at her with no smile. "I was afraid I would not be wanted."

"You will always be welcome in this house," she said. "And it would not be Wintermoon without you. Come in."

"I must go stable the horses," he said. "But you could help me carry in my packages first, if you like."

The others were spilling out of the front door now, calling out Thomas's name in excited voices. "Let Reed carry them," Fiona said with a smile. "He's the strongest."

"I'll be back within the hour."

It was a strange Wintermoon, but not so sad as Fiona had expected. There was surprising comfort in the mere fact that other people moved through the house, other voices were lifted in the outer rooms. She had put Isadora on a bed in her own room, Angeline upstairs in the guest room, and Thomas on the sofa out front, and they were tripping over each other and their piles of half-woven branches any time more than two of them were awake. But that was fun. Meals were sometimes riotously merry, and the time spent making the wreaths companionable and quiet. Even though only two people in the house were related by blood, they were, in the most important sense, a family; and Fiona had only recently realized how much a family should be cherished.

They plaited their bonfire wreath with oak and rowan and truelove, as well as ribbon and lace from Angeline's stores. Reed contributed a length of twine from one of Robert's warehouses, saying it would represent wealth and commerce. Thomas tied on a strip torn from an old canvas sail and said, "There. Now we'll all go traveling." Fiona added a few leaves of lark's breath, a plant she had brought home from Kate's greenhouse and used to relieve her mother's greatest suffering. For she thought it would be a good thing to have a year without pain, if one could only get such a thing by remembering to wish for it. They threw their wreath on the great fire and watched all their hopes turn incendiary, branding the night sky. Fiona assumed that she was not the only one to silently add her own litany of desires, and wish that they might be fulfilled in the coming year.

They stayed out till dawn, feeding the fire, taking turns going inside to warm up. When they finally went in for good and took to their beds, Fiona found she could not sleep. She listened to Isadora's gentle snoring and thought of her mother and the things that might happen in the year to come. No way to predict, she realized, what the following months might bring. No way to guess if she was now as happy as she would ever be, or if the world held great joys that she would only stumble across by living. There was only this moment, and in this moment, these people, and there would never be any more certainty than that.

She turned on her side. But there were still things to hope for, to reach for, without letting go of what she already possessed. She squeezed her eyes tightly shut and let her fingers close and curl, as if catching on to something that had, until now, stayed just outside her grasp.

Chapter Eleven

lminstra insisted that her granddaughter come stay at the Safe-Keeper's cottage, though neither Reed nor Fiona wanted her. Allison was a cheerful girl, nineteen and big as any peasant's daughter, with a round, smiling face and curly dark hair. She was easy-tempered and good at anything she put her hand to, though she didn't like to think too hard and was always happy to see the workday end.

"She'll learn a lot from you," Elminstra said.

"Yes, and I'm sure I'll like her a great deal, but I—can't she stay at your house and come up in the mornings?" Fiona replied.

Elminstra shook her head. "No one's said anything yet, but people will notice, Fiona! A young man and a young woman living together out here all alone—"

"A young—you mean, Reed and me? But we're brother and sister."

"Not by blood you're not, and everyone knows it," Elminstra said with a certain grimness. "People do unsavory things, and so they think other people do, too, and they wouldn't like to see the Safe-Keeper's daughter and the king's bastard living together in a house without a chaperone. There. You say it's silly and it may be, but that's the truth of it, and Angeline would tell you the same. So fix up a room for Allison, and everything will be fine."

Just spiteful enough to make things a tiny bit difficult for the unwanted guest, Fiona gave Allison the upstairs bedroom and kept the big one downstairs for herself. Allison didn't mind, though. She liked the house, liked the room, liked working in the warm indoor garden that Reed had built for Fiona just off the pantry. She liked the meals Fiona cooked, liked the laughter Reed brought to the dinner table. It was, in turn, impossible not to like Allison, and the three of them grew to be fast friends within a fortnight.

Reed was gone most days, having taken a job down at the tavern, now run by his old friend Dirk. He did a little brewing, but mostly waited tables, and came back every week or so with an extra loaf of bread or a pheasant pie that was left over after all the guests had been served. Elminstra often joined them for dinner, bringing a side dish or a fresh-baked cake. All in all, late winter was a much more convivial season for Fiona than early winter had been.

She started to have more visitors during the day as well, people who had secrets to tell and dark thoughts to reveal. She had trained Allison to leave the house when these visitors came calling, to put on a cloak and walk out the front door, so guests could see she was leaving the house and would not worry that she was listening at keyholes to words that were hard to utter. Only a few of these visitors were able to pay in any kind of coin, but they all brought something in exchange for the Safe-Keeper's services—a round of cheese, a bolt of fabric, newly laid eggs. Fiona accepted everything with equal civility.

"It must have been an awfully dreadful secret," Allison said happily one night as they ate very fine beefsteaks brought by a caller. "We never had meat this good in my father's house."

Fiona smiled. "Not so bad, as dreadful secrets go."

Reed was grinning. He seemed to have stopped growing taller this winter, though at just over six feet he was already quite tall enough, and now he was starting to fill out. Fiona had realized with a start the other day that they no longer looked alike. She was still very fair, with fine skin and that silky blond hair they had both had as children, but his complexion had darkened and his hair was now a light brown. And she was so much smaller than he was. No wonder the villagers no longer believed they were brother and sister.

"I bet I know who told it and what the secret was," he said.

Fiona raised her brows. "How could you?"

"I was told a secret myself down at the tavern the other day. I didn't think it was so dreadful either."

After dinner, when Allison had walked down to her grandmother's to share some leftover meat, Fiona demanded, "What do you think my secret is?"

Reed was smiling again. "But if it's a secret—"

"*I* can't tell it, but *you* can!"

"Megan Henshaw's father. He's the only one with enough head of cattle to pay you off in beef. And he's thinking about marrying again—a girl as young as his daughter!"

Fiona was at a loss. No one had ever told her what to do if someone guessed the truth of a secret she was holding. But she felt certain that confirming it would be the same as repeating it, so she said, "If that's true, then it won't be a secret much longer. Was Ric Henshaw announcing such things to everyone in the bar?"

Reed shook his head. "Just to me, just after his third or fourth glass of ale. I gather he's not a man who's used to making decisions that come from the heart, and he doesn't know how to think this thing through."

"You'd be amazed," she said dryly, "how many people that describes."

Fiona could tell that Reed enjoyed his job at the tavern, because Reed liked people and he liked to be in constant motion, but she could also tell that it was starting to pall within a couple of months. So she was not at all surprised, when spring first made a few feints at greenery, to find him impatient to try something new.

"The copper mines?" she asked him one day when she found him restlessly chopping more wood than they would need for the next two months. "The great ships at Merendon? What's calling you now?"

He laid aside his ax and gave her a rueful grin. "There's a horse breeder in Thrush Hollow," he said. "He was at the tavern a week ago. Said he'd train me if I wanted to come out."

"Did you warn him that you wouldn't stay?"

"I did tell him that I'd like to try a variety of jobs before I settle into any particular one."

"I've never even seen you so much as unhitch Thomas's wagon."

"No, but, see, that's why I want to learn!" he said eagerly. "I've never been around horses! I might find I like them better than anything. But I won't know unless I go there and find out."

"Just as long as you're here at Summermoon," she said.

"Oh, I'll be back to visit a dozen times before then. You'll scarcely realize I'm gone."

But she did realize it. His absence emptied the house, made even Allison's cheerfulness seem whispery quiet. There were distractions, of course, foremost among them being spring itself, with its demands of digging and planting and watering. Fiona found Allison's willing energy much more useful than she'd expected to, and the two of them dug a bigger garden than Fiona had been able to maintain in the past. Elminstra visited every few days, exclaiming with envy and offering some of her own cuttings.

"We'll become the showplace of the southern region," Elminstra predicted. "People will journey for a hundred miles to buy herbs and potions from us."

"I might make more money from this than from Safe-Keeping," Fiona said with a smile.

"Well, a late freeze can ruin a garden, and a drought can burn it, so there's no real safe money in planting," Elminstra said. "But people will always have secrets, no matter what the season."

That turned out to be even truer than Fiona had expected, for she was busier during spring than she had been all six months before. She thought some of it had to do with the fact that people in Tambleham were beginning to trust her, to realize that she had not repeated any of the details told to her so far, and they were bringing to her secrets they might have otherwise taken to a Safe-Keeper in Thrush Hollow or Marring Cross. Or perhaps they were too busy, now that it was time to plant crops and breed livestock and make repairs on the barn, to travel so far just to relieve their minds of pressing burdens.

Whatever the reason, every week someone came knocking at the door, asking for a little private time with Fiona. Allison seemed perfectly content to continue working in the garden while Fiona served tea in the kitchen. For the most part, the tales were not so shocking, though now and then Fiona was hard-pressed not to react with anger or disgust. Only once, though, was she told a secret that she did not think she would be able to bear.

"Let's go outside and sit under the kirrenberry tree," said her visitor, a thin, tired woman named Janice. "The day is so pretty, and I like to listen to the silence."

So they brought a blanket and sat under the spreading branches and watched the limbs sway and rub together and make absolutely no noise at all.

"My daughter is bearing my husband's child," Janice said with no preamble. "I thought to come to you for a potion that would—that would—make the child go away, but I waited too long and it is too big in her belly now. And then I thought, he will not bother her so much when she is with child. This gives her a little break from him."

Fiona was filled with such rage that it was almost more than she could do to sit there and be quiet. She clenched her hands into fists and listened to the silence of the kirrenberry tree. She wondered if, in their own mute way, the very bark and branches of the tree were screaming in soundless agony.

"How old is your daughter?"

"Going on fifteen."

Fiona thought. "Was she in school when I was? I should know her if she's only a year or two younger than I am."

Janice shook her head. "We kept her at home. But she learned a lot! She can read, because she taught herself, and she can cook and clean. Well, you've seen our house, there right off the road on the south edge of town. A big place, and she can run the whole thing without my help. I've been sickly," Janice added apologetically. "I can't do so much. And I know that's why my husband has turned to Jillian. If I could have done all my duties, he would not have—"

Again, Fiona kept her hands tight and her outrage stilled. "And your own sickness?" she asked quietly. "What is its nature? Perhaps I have some medicines that could help you. I have a little skill with healing."

Janice shook her head and sighed. "Oh, I've had potions and potions. Nothing gives me any strength," she said. Fiona did not have to try too hard to guess at another story: The woman preferred the comfort of helplessness and a make-believe disease to dealing with the harsh realities of her life. Fiona could not keep from directing some of her silent fury at someone so weak.

"When is the baby due?" she asked.

"We think within the next couple of weeks."

"And will your daughter keep it?"

Janice shook her head. "There's a woman in Thrush Hollow who's lost three of her own babies. She's already begged me to let her take my daughter's. And Jillian is more than willing. I'll send her to Thrush Hollow to have the baby when the time comes. She's too young to be raising a child."

She's too young for any of this, Fiona thought, but did not say it. "I'd like to meet your daughter, if I may."

Janice looked alarmed. "You won't tell her I told you, will you? She's a good girl. She knows it's wrong. She doesn't want anyone to know."

"I won't tell her," Fiona said. "I just want to see her. I might be able to give her some advice—on how to stop unwanted babies from coming in the future. She might be glad to know such things."

"Oh, indeed," Janice said gratefully. "She asked me and asked me, but of course I didn't know. Had five children myself, though only the two of them lived."

"Another daughter?" Fiona asked carefully.

"No, no. My son. He's young yet, but he's a good boy."

They talked a while longer, and when Janice left, she seemed comforted and almost light-hearted, as if she had transferred a heavy weight into hands that were strong enough to hold it. Fiona, on the other hand, was burning up as if with fever; she felt that her skin was so hot she could ignite kindling with her touch. She went around back, where Allison was pulling up weeds, and drew a bucket of water from the well. And dumped it over her head.

"Fiona! What—you—are you all right?" Allison cried, and came running over with her trowel in hand. "You look so flushed! Are you sick? Come in and I'll make you some of that soothing tea."

Fiona just shook her head. Her rage was so bright that it distorted her vision; she could not see the garden or Allison's face very clearly. "I don't think tea will soothe me," she said in a very polite voice.

"Was it—did that woman tell you a secret?" Allison asked in a hesitant voice.

For a moment, Fiona was tempted. Tempted to tell Allison, then tell Elminstra, then walk to town and knock on Lacey's door, and repeat the story to everyone in the seamstress's shop. For she didn't know how you destroyed evil except by exposing it, and this, to her mind, was evil incarnate.

But she was a Safe-Keeper. She had sat under the leaves of the kirrenberry tree and accepted a confidence. She would betray Janice and everyone else who had trusted her if she told this story now.

"Are you going into town later today?" Fiona asked instead. "Earlier, you said you thought you might."

Allison nodded and pushed a lock of hair back from her eyes, leaving a streak of dirt across her forehead. "We're low on flour, and there's some mint to sell," she said. "I thought I'd go in today or tomorrow."

"I've got to write a letter to Lowford," Fiona said. "You can post it for me when you go."

Chapter Twelve

obert Bayliss, it turned out, was very happy to get Fiona's letter, and he responded two days later. "Indeed, yes, I know of a position for a young woman who can cook and clean, and is very gentle with an invalid besides," he wrote. "Our own housekeeper left this spring, and Victoria has tried so hard to do the ordinary chores, but you know how fragile she is. I had asked Angeline to be on the lookout for a nice young woman whom I could hire. I'm sure there must be some in Lowford, but I would be happy to give a chance to the unfortunate girl you mentioned. No doubt, as you say, it will be good for her to put some distance between herself and her young man. If they find they truly love each other, he will come look for her. And if they do not, she will do much better in a new place surrounded by fresh faces. Send her to me when she is well enough to travel."

That very afternoon, Janice's daughter came to the Safe-Keeper's cottage. She would have been as thin as her mother if her stomach had not been so big with the child, and her face was narrow and still. Though she smiled when Fiona answered the door, her expression remained watchful. Her pale brown eyes were filled with an unbearable sadness.

"My mother said you wanted to see me?" she said in a polite, hesitant voice.

"Come in, come in—my assistant has gone down the road to her grandmother's, so you and I are the only ones here," Fiona said. "Would you like some tea? Mint—I grow it myself."

"Tea would be fine, thank you, ma'am."

"Oh, no, I'm just Fiona," Fiona said, pouring out two cups of tea. *Ma'am!* She was sixteen—no one called her that! "And your name is Jillian, is that right?"

"Jillian, yes."

Fiona handed over one cup and sat down next to Jillian at the kitchen table. "You'll think I'm very bold," Fiona said, "but I've been wondering if I could meddle in your life a little bit."

Jillian sipped at her tea, and over the rim of her cup, her sad eyes were inquiring. "Ma'am? What do you mean?"

"I ran into your mother the other day, and she mentioned that you were expecting a child, and I got the impression that—well—that you might not want to continue your relationship with the baby's father," Fiona said. It was as hard for her to appear artless as it was for her to throttle rage, but she had a greater incentive for this little act, and she rather thought she was pulling it off nicely. "And I happen to know a very nice couple in Lowford. Robert and Victoria. Robert runs a trading business where my brother works from time to time. Victoria is very sweet, but often ailing, and she cannot do her household chores. I had heard that they were looking for a housekeeper and someone who could also assist Victoria when she needed help bathing or dressing. And I thought—if you wanted to leave Tambleham and move someplace altogether new, I could arrange for you to get this job as housekeeper."

Jillian stared at her, and for a long, tense moment, Fiona thought she would refuse.

"Oh, ma'am," she said, her voice very low, "I would like that so much I can hardly tell you. But I don't know—I'm not sure—"

"It might be hard for your parents to give you up, I know, you being so young," Fiona rattled on. "But I thought—since you're going to Thrush Hollow to have the baby—my brother is working there this summer. And he could take you up to Lowford, no trouble at all. And introduce you to Robert and Victoria, and to my aunt Angeline as well, who lives very close. Your parents wouldn't have to know of it until you were already settled."

Now some expression had come to Jillian's face, hope and a corresponding deep fear, as if hope was an emotion she could not afford to indulge in. "Oh, if I could do that—" she breathed. "I would go anywhere. I'd do any work."

"Then I can write Robert and Victoria? Tell them you've accepted?"

"Yes, but—are you sure? My father will be very angry—"

"I think you'll be safe in Robert's house."

"And how will your brother know me? And what if he

151

does not want to take me so far? I have no money to pay him—"

Fiona waved a dismissive hand. "Reed goes to Lowford all the time! Angeline feeds him and Robert fusses over him. He won't expect payment."

"And you—why would you be so kind to me?" Jillian whispered. "For I can pay you nothing either."

Fiona leaned forward and put her hand over the girl's free hand, trembling where it lay on the table. "Because there are all kinds of trouble in the world, and most of them I can't fix, but I saw a way to fix this predicament," she said. "I can't make the baby go away, and I can't make your— make your young man go away, but I can help you move someplace that might be a little easier. And sometime, someday, you may see a young girl who needs your help, and you'll find a way to give her aid. That's the only payment I would think to ask."

"And I'll do it," Jillian said.

Fiona sat back. "Now. We must plan what you will need to take with you. When are you going to Thrush Hollow?"

They plotted for the next hour, discussing how many of her clothes she could bring with her without making her parents suspicious, and what she might need to take from the house if she was never to return to it. It was an amazing thing, Fiona thought. The girl seemed to change and brighten as they sat there, grow sweeter and more buoyant with every scheme that they unfolded. It was only when Allison came through the front door and called out a greeting that they finally rose to their feet, satisfied with their plans.

"I'll write Reed tonight, and my aunt Angeline," Fiona said. "You'll see. Everything will go without a hitch."

And it did. A week later, Jillian was in Thrush Hollow, and two days after that, was delivered of a healthy, furious baby girl. Three days later, Reed drove her to Lowford and took her straight to the Bayliss house. Robert wrote Fiona once she'd been there a week to tell her how attached Victoria had grown to the young lady, how pleased they all were with her quiet, helpful presence in their house. Jillian wrote also, in a clear, painstaking hand, a letter that said merely "thank you thank you thank you thank you" until it filled nearly an entire sheet. At the end of it, she wrote, "I will do what you asked whenever I can."

Janice came back to the Safe-Keeper's cottage when Jillian had been gone a month, this time with a trivial secret about a spasm of envy that had led her to deliberately tear a friend's gown. When Fiona could contain her curiosity no longer, she asked casually, "Your daughter. Has she had her baby yet?"

Janice nodded mournfully. "I suppose so. She went off to Thrush Hollow, like I told you she would, but she never came back. My husband went to look for her, but she was gone and no one knew where. I can't say I'm sorry, because I think she's probably someplace better, but I can't imagine where she'd get to. She didn't have two coins to rub together and no friends to help her. I just hope she's not dead in a ditch somewhere. I suppose my husband might be eyeing the serving girls down at the tavern now, but I don't mind that so much. I do miss Jillian, though."

And Fiona realized she had been successful in her entire strategy—she had rescued Jillian and left no traces behind. Janice did not suspect her; no one knew the truth. She had not compromised her role as Safe-Keeper and yet she had lived up to the higher ideals of human goodness. She was so pleased with herself she smiled at Janice with a great deal more kindness than the woman deserved.

A few weeks later, she was to discover she had not been quite so careful as she believed. Thomas arrived in Tambleham and stopped for afternoon tea at the cottage. Allison came in to meet him and did not seem at all intimidated by his measuring eyes and blunt way of speaking.

"Don't be too nice to him," Fiona warned her, cutting them all pieces of lemon cake. "He'll say something hurtful the minute you relax your guard."

Allison laughed good-naturedly. "Oh, what will he tell me that I haven't already heard? I'm too big, I'm too loud, I look like a cow. If you grow up with brothers, you don't have too many illusions about yourself."

Thomas was watching her with a quizzical smile. "You're cheerful and kind, and no one who knows you dislikes you," he said. "You bring the rare gift of happiness with you everywhere you go."

Allison nearly choked on her tea. "I thought you said he would be mean to me!" she exclaimed to Fiona.

Fiona stirred her own tea. "Maybe I'm the only one he's ever mean to."

"No, usually I'm mean to everyone," he said. "But I never say anything untrue."

"The truth is often unkind," Fiona said.

"But the truth is real," he said. "That gives it great value."

Allison finished the last of her cake and stood up. "Well, I'm sure you two have a lot to talk over," she said. "I'll go work in the garden."

Thomas, smiling again, watched her go. "Not a bad choice at all if you're going to have someone foisted on you," he said.

Fiona laughed. "How do you know I didn't ask for her to be my companion?"

"Elminstra told me. But she was right, of course. You can't live here all alone with Reed."

"Since Reed is very rarely here, it is not really a concern."

"But villagers love to gossip. And you, my devious young Safe-Keeper, will have to be very, very careful not to give them food for discussion."

Fiona sipped her tea. "What can you possibly mean?"

He pointed at her. "It was clever. I would not have pieced it together except for something that Reed let slip. But you have engineered some kind of salvation mission for a young girl named Jillian."

Fiona gave him a limpid look. "I have no idea what you're talking about."

Thomas ticked off the points on his fingers. "A young girl from Tambleham delivers a child in Thrush Hollow. She takes a job in Lowford. You have arranged all this."

Fiona shrugged. "She needed a job. Robert needed a serving girl. I brought them together. I see nothing mysterious in that."

"It is clear she is running from someone or something quite odious in Tambleham. If I were to guess I would say she is escaping the attentions of a father or a brother or an uncle. And that you were told of these sins, and you could not bear them."

"But you don't know this for truth," she said.

"But I don't know this for truth," he repeated. "I would not say the supposition aloud in the marketplace—or tell her parents where she has taken refuge."

"And no secrets have been betrayed, and I do not see what you're making such a fuss about."

He smiled at her. It was the warm smile of a teacher who approves of a very clever student. "I told you once you would never be a Safe-Keeper," he said.

"And I told you you were wrong. I am a very good one."

"Your mother never would have done such a thing, you know," he said. "She would have listened to the secret, and she would have kept it. That is all a Safe-Keeper is required to do."

Fiona poured more tea into her cup. "My mother could live with grief more gracefully than I can. But some of those sorrows weighed very heavily on her. I don't think she would disapprove of what I have done."

"Oh, you're graceful enough," Thomas said. "But you're far too passionate. Now that you have started, you will not be able to stop yourself from wanting to right grave wrongs. You do not want to keep secrets. You want to enact justice."

"I might be able to do both," she said.

He laughed. "What a crusader you would have been! You

should have been the daughter of a Truth-Teller, not a Safe-Keeper." He took a drink of tea. "Then again," he added, "perhaps you are."

"Perhaps I am," she said, "but not yours."

He tilted his head to one side. "So you know that secret, do you?"

She nodded. "My mother told me before she died."

"And have you told your father?"

"Not yet. I don't know that I ever will."

"Did your mother forbid you to repeat it?"

"No, but she said I would want to hold this knowledge for a while yet. And having thought about it a long time, I realize she is right."

"Do you know the name of Reed's father as well?"

She shook her head. "That she didn't tell me."

"I wonder if Angeline knows. She was there that night, after all, and she took him from the traveler's arms."

Fiona laughed. "If I had to guess, I would say that Angeline knows who my father is, but does not know Reed's for certain."

Thomas smiled. "Well, your father may indeed be the greater mystery, but I would agree that Angeline can solve it. She and your mother were very close."

"And they shared many secrets," Fiona agreed.

"As you and Reed share all secrets."

"Except this one," she replied.

Fiona was surprised at how much she enjoyed Thomas's visit; he had always annoyed her before. But now it was like having a piece of her old life back, a memory of her mother. He reminded her of a prickly old uncle who could, when he chose, be extraordinarily benevolent. She could tell that he was pleased with her handling of Jillian's situation, and this gave her a certain measure of pride. The only other person with whom she would be able to share all the details of the case would be Angeline who, like Thomas, had probably already guessed. Angeline might not approve, but it was good to know that Thomas did.

Summermoon came, and Reed with it. Fiona and Reed and Allison walked down to the village for the fair, and Reed got free lemonade for them from Dirk's tavern. There were jugglers and pipers and children running wildly through the streets, garlanded with flowers, and the whole festival was very merry. But Fiona preferred the dark, still, thoughtful time of Wintermoon, with its stark contrasts of frost and fire.

"I'm going to Lowford in a few weeks," Reed told her as he packed up to return to Thrush Hollow. "Robert needs me."

"What about the horses?"

He rolled his eyes. "Big and dumb and more willful than you," he said. "I was never as patient as I needed to be. The breeder told me I needed to learn to love them, but I—well, I never did. At least I understand Robert's charts and boxes."

"And you're bored."

He grinned. "And I'm bored. Time for a change."

"How long in Lowford this time?"

"I don't know. A few months. Robert won't expect me any longer than that."

She stood on tiptoe to kiss him on the cheek. "I don't care where you go or what you do," she said, "as long as you're back by Wintermoon."

He returned the kiss in kind. "Always," he said. And he was gone.

Chapter Thirteen

he next few months followed a very similar pattern, except that Allison began courting. So sometimes she would bring company home for dinner, and sometimes she would be out late at night, but she was always back in the house, alone, by midnight. Ed was a shy and not very articulate young farmer who seemed to think Safe-Keepers were as wondrous as princesses, but Fiona thought he was a very good choice for Allison. He adored her, for one thing; he could not keep his eyes from following her when she walked or gestured. He was tall, for another, and big-boned, and she looked just the right size when she was standing beside him. And he seemed as gentle-hearted as she was, which would be the one thing Fiona would wish for her. So she made him welcome when he came to the house, and hoped that true love would triumph.

Other than that, very little changed. People came to her door to confide secrets that were shameful or ridiculous or surprising, but none of them moved Fiona the way Jillian's story had, and so she made no attempts at intervention.

Summer slipped away and the autumn harvests kept Fiona and Allison busy, drying herbs and canning vegetables. Reed and Angeline came to town for a few days to celebrate Fiona and Reed's birthday, and then reappeared at Wintermoon, Isadora and Thomas right behind them. It was the second Wintermoon they had celebrated without Damiana, and though they talked of her frequently and with great affection, the loss was not so severe this time; the memories were good.

Reed had news: He had decided to take a job up north, with a merchant trader whom Robert knew. "I might be gone two months or more," he warned Fiona, "if I actually go out on one of the ships."

"Then let me know if you leave and when you're back," she said.

"It's a difficult life," Thomas commented. "You won't like it."

Reed shrugged. "I don't mind hard work."

"No, but you won't like this."

"If you go someplace exotic, bring us all back jewels," Isadora said. "Opals or black pearls or emeralds."

"I hate to think of you aboard a ship," Angeline said. "So far away in the middle of so much water—how can I ever think you're safe?"

Reed laughed. "I'll be fine, I promise you."

"He'll come back home," Fiona said. "He always does."

Nonetheless, she was sad when he left, and, like Angeline, worried about him being on an oceangoing vessel; there seemed to be no margin of safety at all in such a venture. But she worked in her indoor garden, and made dinner for Allison and Ed, and gravely heard out secrets, and watched the white winter months tiptoe past. And then it was spring again, and all the flowers were blooming, and she got a letter from Reed saying he would be home within the week. He had hated being on board ship, he had been frequently sick and dreadfully lonely, and even the chance to see foreign shores did not erase his misery. "Though I have seen some beautiful places and have so many little trinkets for all of you that I think even Isadora will approve," he wrote.

Indeed, when he showed up six days later, he was loaded down with treasures—jade carvings, ivory horns, mother-of-pearl hair pins, onyx beads. Allison loved them all, so Fiona let her choose first from the cache, and then saved the rest for the next time the others would visit.

"Where now?" she asked Reed one afternoon as they walked down to the streambed. It was hot for spring and they had decided, with a minimum of discussion, to cut short their chores for the day and head out to familiar haunts. "Merendon? Wodenderry? Lowford again?"

"Here, I think, for a while at least," he said, slipping off his shoes and stepping into the water. "Ow! That's *cold!* You don't want to get in."

"I do," she said, and splashed in beside him. Her feet were instantly numb with the shock. "But not for very long."

He was obviously determined to stand it as long as she could, so he bent over and plunged his hand wrist-deep in the water, and emerged with a rock between his fingers. "I'll work at the tavern for a month or two while I decide what I want to do next."

She smiled. "If you ever do decide."

He sent the stone skipping down the undulating surface of the water. "I'm not like you. I wasn't born knowing. I have to keep trying new things till I find the one that fits."

"Don't you have any—any real dreams?" she asked. "Something you think about all the time, something you'd do if you could only figure out how?"

He shook his head and dug for another stone. "Nothing. It all looks interesting to me, at least for a while. And there's nothing I'm missing, nothing I really want." He was quiet for a moment, standing very still with the stone caught in his curled hand. "Well, two things I'd wish for, but I can't do anything about them."

"What two things?" she asked. Her feet were so cold her whole body was starting to shiver, but she was not about to climb out of the stream now.

He tossed the rock and it made a series of graceful landings along the top of the water before sinking out of sight. "I wish I knew who my father was, for one."

"I'd tell you, if I knew," she said. "But I don't. What's the second thing?"

He smiled and shook his head. "Some other time."

She waited, but he only teased out more rocks and bounced them down the water. "I'm freezing," she exclaimed, and clambered out onto the bank. She had to sit with her legs crossed and her icy toes tucked into the backs of her knees until her feet warmed up enough that she could feel to put her shoes back on. Reed stayed in the water a few minutes longer, just so it was clear who was not afraid of the cold, then climbed out beside her. Barefoot, he stretched out on the bank and looked up at the cloudless sky, a delicate blue that looked ready to fade at the first sign of sunset.

"At any rate," she said, "I'm glad you're home. For now."

Isadora came by a few weeks later and happily picked through Reed's store of treasures. "Ah, if no one else wants this little jade pendant, that's what I'll have," she said. "Look at that. Did you ever see such a color? It looks like the water in the pond by my mother's house just under the shade of the elm tree. Mysterious and full of things. Reed, you can buy gifts for me any time."

She stayed a week and seemed very tired, so Fiona made her sit in the garden and do nothing but watch the flowers stretch their petals to the sun. When her own chores were done and Allison was off with her young man, Fiona sat beside the Dream-Maker and listened to the tales of her travels.

"Where are you going when you leave Tambleham?" Fiona asked.

"Wodenderry. Which reminds me, didn't you have some young girl here you wanted me to take an interest in?"

Fiona had almost forgotten. "Megan! Yes. Why, have you found someone who wants a companion?"

"Well, if nothing else, I thought *I* might like someone to travel with me. She could stay with me as long as she liked, and if she found a position with someone else in the city, all well and good. And if not, I'd either buy her a passage back home or let her travel on with me. If I liked her," Isadora added. "If she's whiny or puts on airs, I won't be able to abide her very long."

Fiona grinned. "I haven't seen Megan in a few months. She comes by now and then for the herbs I can sell her, and she hasn't seemed so determined to get away. In fact, I think they're planning their wedding for next spring, so she might not be so willing to go. But I'll ask her."

Megan, when she arrived at the Safe-Keeper's cottage the next day, was in transports at the idea of traveling anywhere in Isadora's company, particularly to the royal city. "To Wodenderry with the Dream-Maker!" she exclaimed. "Yes! Oh, yes! When do we leave? Do I have time to go home and pack?"

Isadora was laughing. "Two days from now was what I planned. That should give you ample time, I think."

"How early in the morning will we leave? Should I sleep here the night before?"

"Goodness, no. I'm an old woman. I don't believe in hauling my bones out of bed before dawn."

"Megan, what will you say to your father?" Fiona asked practically. "And to Cal? Or do you not plan to tell them?"

She tossed her pretty dark hair. "I'll tell them. But once they know I'm in company with Isadora, they'll be very happy to have me go. They both have plans and schemes that they'd like to see come true. They'll think I'll have a chance to put in a good word for them."

Isadora looked faintly alarmed. "It doesn't work that way, you know—I wish it did, sometimes."

Megan laughed. She sounded more girlish than she ever

165

had during any of the other times she'd come to Fiona's cottage. "I know that," she said. "But I won't tell them."

Isadora left with Megan; Reed stayed behind. Once again, he took up his old job at the tavern, and once again, Fiona thought how his presence brought warmth and joy to the little cottage. Allison's young man was not so shy when Reed was around, so the four of them enjoyed several convivial evenings, playing games, telling stories, and laughing till their ribs protested. Now and then Elminstra's grandson Greg—Allison's cousin—would join them, bringing the young lady he was courting. The six of them had their own private Summermoon festival and stayed up all night talking, just as if it had been the winter holiday. None of them got any real work done the next day, though Fiona and Allison had a day's worth of planting ahead of them, and Greg and Reed had real jobs to go to. Greg's young lady lay on the sofa all day, complaining of a headache, but she revived by dinnertime when Greg came back to fetch her. In fact, they all found themselves in a social mood by then, so they made a meal out of leftovers and celebrated the first day of midsummer.

"This was the best Summermoon ever," Reed said that night as they stood at the gate and waved good-bye to the departing couple.

"This is what I love about living in the village," Fiona replied.

"Oh, and you have to love the village gossip as well," he said as they turned back to the house. "Did you hear about

Ned's daughter? The one who married Josh's grandson?"

Stepping up on the porch while he stayed on the walkway, Fiona turned to frown at him. "Did I hear what, exactly?" she said.

"The child she just bore. Not her husband's after all."

This was a secret Fiona had heard from the errant wife herself, who had sobbed out the story one afternoon in Fiona's kitchen. "Who told you this tale?" she asked quietly.

Reed's eyebrows rose. "Am I not supposed to know? I didn't tell anyone else. I never do repeat the things anyone tells me—except to you, of course. I tell you everything. You already know everything."

"But who told you this?" she insisted.

"She did. A few days ago. She'd come to the tavern to buy her family's dinner for the evening because she said she didn't have the energy to make a meal. I thought, well, you have enough energy to walk to town, but I think she meant she can't bring herself to pretend to care for someone she hates, and making his dinner means she cares for him. You know?"

"Yes, I understand," Fiona said softly. "I just—I wonder—"

He shrugged. "Sometimes people tell me things. I think it's because of our mother. They think I understand how to keep silent—and I do. But sometimes I wish they didn't choose me to talk to."

She smiled and went in. Allison and her beau had gone down to Elminstra's for the evening, so it was just the two of them for a change. "Sit down while I get dinner," she said. "Tell me what other secrets you know."

The report took some time, and some of the revelations surprised her; they were such emotional stories that she had not thought the tellers would be able to recite them more than once. One or two were stories that she did not already know, but she did not tell Reed that. She didn't want him to think he was betraying a confidence.

"Dirk says people who have been drinking often choose to pour their woes into the barkeeper's ear, and he says he's glad I'm the one who hears them these days," Reed finished up. "But sometimes I think he never heard any stories like the ones I've been told."

"I wouldn't be surprised if you're right," Fiona said. "But you have to honor the secrets. You have to be as silent as a kirrenberry tree."

He smiled at her. "As silent as you."

It wasn't till after they'd celebrated their birthday that Reed grew fidgety again. Fiona was on the watch for the signs, for she knew he could never stay in one place long, and she was braced for the announcement when it came. But she found she was, after all, not nearly as well prepared for it as she'd thought.

He said nothing till they were alone one night, Allison and Ed having walked down to Elminstra's for the evening. She was putting away the clean dishes, and he was stacking more firewood beside the stove. Then he turned to her and said, in a tone of great resolution, "Fiona."

She didn't even bother to turn from the cabinet. "Where to this time?" she said.

There was a moment's silence, and then he laughed. "How do you always know?"

"I can read you the way I read the shape of my own name on a piece of paper," she said quietly. "There's somewhere else you want to be."

"No, not exactly—I *want* to be here, but I think—I have—there are so many other things I need to do first," he said.

She kept her back to him. "What things?" she said. "Shovel horse manure? Get sick on a merchant ship?"

He gave a soft laugh. "It's true, neither of those turned out exactly as I'd hoped—"

"And where are you off to now? To bury yourself in a copper mine and find you don't like the dark? To work in a mill to discover you don't like breathing in flour dust the whole day long?"

"I want to go to the royal city," he said quietly.

Now she turned to look at him, astonishment on her face. "And why?"

He looked defensive but determined, a big, fair-haired, sweet-natured, restless young man whom no one had ever been able to deter or direct. "I want to see my father."

"You don't even know if he is your father!"

"Everyone says he is—everyone believes it."

"And you will do—what? Walk up to him? Introduce yourself? Say, 'I'm your bastard son, will you allow me to come to court?'"

"No—I don't think so—I don't know! It's just that—my whole life—everyone has always thought, everyone has always looked at me like I was a royal bastard. Perhaps I am. Perhaps I'm not! But maybe if I *know*, once and for all, if I see him and I can tell—"

"Then what?" she demanded. She was blazingly furious and did not even know why. "He will invite you to court? He will name you his heir? Is *that* what you really expect? Is that why you can't settle down in Tambleham or Lowford?"

"No, of course not. Fiona, I want to *know*, can't you understand that?" He flung his hands out and took a few paces around the kitchen, so big and so agitated he seemed to fill the whole room. "I don't have any idea who I am! Who was my mother? Who was my father? Who am I supposed to be?"

"I never knew who my father was, either, but I never questioned who *I* was supposed to be," she answered. "It's not like we were missing out on any love. You and I were raised by the same woman. The same friends and family cared for us."

"Yes, but they were *your* family—they were related to you by blood," he pointed out. "I showed up in the middle of the night, dressed in silence and secrets, and everything that I have become I have had to fashion for myself. I want to know what life I was *supposed* to lead, what I was born for. It might not be a life I would choose, but shouldn't I know where I was destined to belong?"

Now she was even more angry. "There comes a point in every man's life where it does not matter who his parents were—yes, and in every woman's life, too! You are a strong man or a weak one because of your own experiences and

170

your own heart, not because someone else's blood runs in your veins. You are kind or cruel for the same reasons. You might be the king's legitimate son and be a man I would not care to know, or the child of a peasant laborer and be the most beloved man in five kingdoms. Your father's rank might determine some privileges, but it is your own soul that determines who you are."

He was shaking his head, adamant and unyielding. "You don't understand. It is different for you."

"I do understand, and it is no different," she snapped. "But nothing I say will stop you. Go to Wodenderry! Meet the king! Then come back and tell me what you've learned."

He looked at her, his eyes narrowed. "Why are you so angry? What is it you think I'm going to find?"

She turned away, suddenly weary. "I am angry if you value yourself only at your birthright, and I think you'll find—I think you'll find more questions than answers."

"Then I'll come back here, as I always do," he said softly, "and see if the answers are in Tambleham."

She didn't look at him. "And if the answers are in Wodenderry?"

"I'll come back here anyway. Always. Or wherever it is you are."

He left two days later. Fiona felt the loss of his presence even more deeply this time; for the first few days, the house was almost unlivable. When Allison and Ed were not around, the silence was too severe for her to endure, so she would go down to Elminstra's or all the way to town just to have company. One day, she and Elminstra made a little excursion of the trip, going to Lacey's shop to order new bolts of fabric, then having a noon meal at Dirk's tavern.

"I don't know if she's had a chance to tell you yet," Elminstra said, as they ate their bread and cheese and drank glasses of pressed apple juice. "But Allison and Ed have decided to marry in the spring."

Fiona felt herself come alive with the first real smile she'd managed since Reed left for Wodenderry. "But that's wonderful news!" she exclaimed. "I like him so much."

"We've been trying to decide where they should live," Elminstra went on. "She has become so attached to you and your garden that she does not want to move far from you. Ed's father had wanted him to take over his land, but Ed's no farmer. He's been working for Ned in town doing blacksmithing, and he likes that much better. So if they lived on my property, or somewhere near it, she could be close to you and he could get easily to town."

Fiona laughed a little ruefully. "Yes, of course, once they're married Allison won't be living with me any longer. I was too happy for her too soon! Now I don't want her to marry after all."

Elminstra laughed too. "Well, I have plenty of grandchildren I can summon to come be your companions," she said. "You need never be lonely as long as my daughters keep producing daughters of their own."

Fiona shrugged. "I am eighteen now, and I don't think I need someone to guard me from solitude any longer," she said.

"I disagree! Eighteen and a small blond slip of a thing!

Who entertains desperate characters every day! There is no chance I would allow you to live in that house alone."

Fiona waved a hand. "But we were talking about Allison and Ed! Do you actually have room on your property to build them a cottage?"

"No, but my house is much larger than yours, and I'm getting old enough to feel it. I've been thinking about having one of my grandchildren move in with me to take over some of the care of the house and land. Allison and Ed could live with me, and then have the house after I'm gone."

"You won't be gone for years and years and *years*, so don't talk that way," Fiona said, a little alarmed. "I have a better plan, I think. The land across the road from me belongs to Angeline—did you know that?"

Elminstra squinted. "Now that you mention it, I do remember Damiana saying that once or twice."

"Their mother owned all the property, long before the road came through. My mother kept the house when my aunt moved to Lowford, but the rest of the land belongs to Angeline. She might be willing to sell it to Allison and Ed— or, if not, rent it to them and let them build on the property. It will do her no harm to have a little income."

"I must say, I like this idea very much," Elminstra said. "And for you to have Allison and Ed live so close to you—I like that even better."

"So close I will not need a companion in the house with me," Fiona said with a smile.

"Ah, now *that* I did not agree to!" the old witch said, and they both laughed, and toasted each other with juice.

That afternoon, Fiona made a white cake with white frosting and had it waiting when Allison came home from an outing with her betrothed.

"You know! My grandmother told you!" Allison cried, and Fiona laughed and hugged her. "Oh, I've been so afraid to tell you, for I feel like I'm abandoning you and I would never do that—"

"Allison, you are not abandoning me! Even if you and Ed packed up and moved to the other side of the country, I would not feel that way. You have been such a good friend to me for so long. I would not begrudge you the tiniest moment of happiness. How could you think that—"

Allison sniffled. "But you're all alone and I have so much."

Fiona smiled. "I have a great deal as well. Never think that I do not feel surrounded by love."

So they ate the white cake and talked about weddings and decided that between the two of them, they could make Allison's dress. Though they might get Lacey's help with any fancy trim. Fiona mentioned her scheme about renting them the land directly across from the cottage, and Allison nearly jumped out of her chair with delight.

"And I'll put in my *own* garden, and between us we'll have every herb or healing plant in the whole kingdom, and people will travel from every city to buy from us," Allison said.

"We will be famous farther afield than this kingdom," Fiona said loftily. "Next time Reed signs up to be a sailor, we'll make him bring back marvelous cuttings from foreign lands. No one in three kingdoms will have gardens as fine as ours."

"Have you heard from Reed?" Allison asked.

"Oh, he writes every few days."

There was a pause. "And has he met King Marcus?" Allison asked next.

Fiona laughed. "Not yet. But knowing Reed, he might actually find a way."

"And what will happen then, do you think?"

Fiona shook her head. "I cannot even guess."

Chapter Fourteen

Right before the weather turned cold, Angeline traveled to town. She quickly agreed to lease her land to Allison and Ed, and she warmly wished them well, but she had more serious matters on her mind.

"Victoria Bayliss is very ill," she said gravely. "Kate has been there every day with some new potion, but nothing she tries has had any effect. I know that you have some cuttings that come from no other garden, and I wondered if you might have something we could try. Robert is so sad. He sits by her bedside night and day."

"Most of what I have you can find in Kate's gardens as well, but I have one or two herbs that might be unfamiliar to her," Fiona said. "Is it lung trouble? Stomach disease? Is there any pain? If nothing else, I probably have a tonic or two that will let her rest in comfort."

"It is lung trouble, stomach trouble, pain—it is everything," Angeline said. "I am very afraid she will die."

"Well, I'm sorry for it," Fiona said, though she was not really sorry. She had never been able to bring herself to care too much for the helpless, clinging Victoria. "Is Jillian still keeping their house?"

Angeline nodded, smiling a little. "Such a quiet and generous girl. Victoria has treated her like a daughter, and everyone who meets her simply loves her. I don't know—" Angeline shook her head. "If Victoria dies, Jillian cannot continue living in Robert's house, of course. But there are many places she could go in Lowford. Kate would take her in, as would I, and there are friends of Robert's who could use a good worker."

"She mustn't come back here," Fiona said.

Angeline shook her head. "No, I don't think she ever will."

Winter crept in one night and laid its pale hand over the world while they were sleeping. They woke to a glittering scene of frost and thoughts of Wintermoon.

Letters from Isadora, Reed, and Thomas promised that they would arrive in time for the holiday. "Listen to this," Fiona said to Allison, amused, as she skimmed through a missive from the Dream-Maker. "Megan has found a patron! A rich older woman who needs a companion to accompany her to court! Isadora says the older woman is vain and pompous but somehow related to the king—a cousin, perhaps?—and that Megan is beside herself with rapture." Fiona looked up, smiling. "So Isadora has made Megan's dream come true, it seems."

"Do you think she'll ever be back to marry Cal Seston?" Allison asked.

Fiona laughed. "The minute she left this town for Wodenderry was the last time Cal was ever going to see that girl."

"I can't help but be pleased by that," Allison said. "Cal was always a nasty boy."

"And I think she was only going to marry him because their fathers wanted to join the land," Fiona said.

"But didn't her father just marry that girl? The one practically Megan's age?"

Fiona nodded. "And wouldn't you think she'd be producing children of her own soon enough? She'll probably be just as glad if the wedding's called off."

Allison laughed and spread her hands. "See? Everything always works out for the best."

The weather grew bitterly cold and the first snowfall came weeks before Wintermoon. While the weather was so bad, construction halted on the cottage being built across the road. Nonetheless, Fiona and Allison went over every day to take a look, strolling through the exposed bones of the house, the ribs of the internal rooms, the templed fingers of the beamed ceiling. This would be the main room, this the kitchen, this a bedroom. Out back, where a layer of snow now covered the wild weeds and knotted undergrowth, would be the garden, half vegetables and half herbs. If there was time for roses, they would be planted at the gate.

"And I'll give you some truelove," Fiona said, "so you'll have everything you want."

Fiona had most everything she wanted when, two days

after the snow sifted down, Reed arrived. He jumped from the back of a stranger's cart, flipped the man a coin and called a out a word of thanks, and rushed up the walk to where Fiona stood waiting.

"I wasn't expecting you for another week!" she exclaimed, hugging as much of his big frame as she was able. "How are you? Where's Isadora? Why did you come back early?"

"Homesick," he said. "I wanted to be with you."

"Come in. You must be freezing. I'll make you some tea."

He followed her into the house. "Where's Allison?"

"Down at Elminstra's. Did you see the house when you pulled up? It's going to be charming. We'll walk over and inspect it once you've warmed up."

"It'll be strange having neighbors so close," he remarked, sprawling in one of the kitchen chairs.

"But neighbors I'll be happy to have," she said.

She served hot tea and leftover tarts, and he ate as enthusiastically as if he hadn't stopped for lunch on the road, which he'd already admitted he had. She watched him covertly, to see if there were signs of strain or exhaustion on his face, but he seemed, as always, happy and at ease.

"So! Tell me about the royal city," she said. "How was Isadora doing? Did you meet the king?"

"Isadora—oh, there's a story there—Isadora's just fine. No, I never met the king, but I saw him more than once."

"How did you manage that?"

"Oh, well, every time he left the palace he would ride out in an entourage. The streets would be lined with people, common folk just waiting for a glimpse of royalty. There would be the king, guards in a ring all around him, riding his black horse and sitting as straight as you please, gazing directly before him."

"And what did you think of him?"

Reed considered. "Well, of course, it's hard to tell much just from watching a man ride by on horseback. But I thought he seemed very stern. He never smiled. Sometimes he would wave, or toss a few coins, particularly to the children. But he did not look like a warm man. He did not look like someone who had experienced much affection."

"He's dark, people say."

Reed nodded. "Oh yes, the blackest of hair, though it's starting to go gray now. He keeps it cropped fairly short and he wears a small silver crown when he goes out. Very elegant. But he—" Reed shrugged.

Fiona stirred her tea. "Did you think he looked like you?"

"No!" he burst out. "That's what I was going to say! He doesn't look at all like me! Not just the color of his hair, but the shape of his mouth and the slope of his nose—all of it was wrong. None of it was familiar. Fiona, I don't think he is my father after all."

She lifted her cup and sipped the hot liquid. "And what do you think of that?" she said neutrally.

He spread his hands upon the table. "I don't know what to think! My whole life people have said—but I don't think it's true! So then, well, it's even more confusing. My father could have been anyone. Anyone! It makes me feel very strange. Untethered, almost." He shook his head. "But I wasn't really disappointed. I mean, I didn't look at him and think, 'Oh, I wish I belonged to that man.' I was just as glad I didn't. I just wished—well, it would be good to know whom I did belong to."

"You belong to me," she said, "and Angeline and Thomas and Elminstra and all of us. As you always have. Nothing has changed."

"Yes," he said. "Though it seems to have changed a little bit. I can't exactly explain."

Fiona took another swallow. "So! Did you see Princess Lirabel? What was she like?"

Reed sat forward, excited enough to forget his own mysteries. "I almost *met* the princess," he said. "It was the most amazing thing."

"No! What happened?"

"I had gone to visit Isadora—she rented a little suite very close to the palace, and it was much nicer than mine, so I would go by every few days to have tea with her. And she would tell me stories of this rich lady and that great lord who would come by her rooms in stealth and open their hearts to her. 'Can you believe that people as grand as these have such dreams?' she said to me once."

"Well, and what sort of dreams?"

"Oh, there were the ones you might expect—the woman who would beg to bear a son for her husband, the man who would ask for wealth. But sometimes—well, Isadora told me that one woman said all she wanted was to go live in the country, as far from the palace as possible. Another one sat

181

there and cried, wishing her mother would love her. I mean, it might have been anybody from Tambleham or Thrush Hollow sitting there. The things they wanted so badly were sometimes the most simple things."

"And how did you meet the princess?"

"I was there having tea with Isadora, and we heard this commotion on the steps. And Isadora said, 'Oh my goodness, that's someone come here to ramble on about a dream. Would you mind hiding in the other room? This shouldn't take long.' So I stepped into her bedroom, but I kept the door open a tiny bit because I—well, I wanted to see some of these grand folks for myself."

Fiona grinned. "I'd have done the same thing."

"And who came through the door but three guards in palace livery, and this young woman dressed in so much velvet and gold that I thought she could not be real. The guards said nothing, but the woman minced over to Isadora and said in this very haughty voice, 'My lady is wishful of a few moments of your time, if you could see her now.' And I didn't know who 'my lady' was, but Isadora did, for I could see her hands trembling a little. 'Yes, yes, I will see the princess any time she likes,' Isadora said. And I thought, 'The princess!' And the next moment Lirabel came through the door."

"What did she look like?"

"Well, her face was very heavily veiled at first. 'Go, all of you,' she said, and her lady-in-waiting protested, but eventually the lot of them cleared out and closed the door behind them. Isadora seemed a little nervous, but not as nervous as

I would have been, and she offered the princess some tea and asked if she wanted to sit down, and pretty soon they were both sitting at Isadora's little table. And the princess pulled her veil back to drink but I didn't get a very good look at her face. I didn't think she looked that much like the king—her mouth was the same, and her coloring, but her face was rounder. And sweeter, if you know what I mean. Her eyes seemed very serious, like she spent all her time thinking."

"And why had she come to see Isadora? I suppose she had a dream to ask about. How strange, that a princess could not just command everything her heart might desire."

"Which is exactly what I thought! Until she began talking, that is. At first she didn't say anything, just sat there drinking her tea and looking grave. And then she looked up at Isadora and said, 'All I want is for my father to accept me as his heir. All I want is for my father to look at me and realize I am his daughter, the legitimate child of his body, the one who will rule after him. Why am I not good enough for him? Is it because I am a woman or because I am *me*? Long ago I stopped wanting him to love me. Now I just want him to publicly acknowledge that I will inherit his throne. Can you make this happen?'"

"Oh, poor Isadora," Fiona murmured.

"I know! Because what happens if you don't grant the wishes of royalty? Do they have your head cut off?"

"What did Isadora say?"

"She was very good. She was very calm. She said, 'Princess, the magic that is in me chooses what it will perform. Sometimes it grants the wishes of beggars in the street; sometimes it involves itself with the dreams of the gentry. I cannot predict it and I cannot control it. I would grant this wish for you if I could. But I can guarantee nothing.'

"And the princess pulled her veil back on and stood up. 'Then no one can help me,' she said. She was out the door almost before Isadora had had time to scramble to her feet. I saw her lady-in-waiting come over and take her hand, and then the door shut, and I heard their footsteps on the stairs."

"Did you come out and have more tea with Isadora?"

"Tea! She had collapsed in her chair and we both felt faint. I poured us each a glass of brandy. It was the middle of the day, mind you, but we didn't care. 'I think it's time for me to be leaving Wodenderry soon,' Isadora finally said. 'I don't think I can endure too many more interviews like that one.'"

Fiona rested her chin on her fist. "I do feel sorry for the princess, though," she said. "Can you imagine? To have lived the way she has for—how old is she now, twenty-eight? To have lived all that time waiting for your fate to be decided. Will I be queen someday? Or will my father keep trying to sire sons who will inherit in my place? And you know all that uncertainty must have affected how everyone at the palace has treated her all these years. Some people would have cultivated her, hoping that she *would* be named heir and that she would then remember their attentions. Others would have shunned her, not wanting the king to think they showed her any favor. Think how bitter and calculating she must be by now."

Reed was staring at her. "Why, Fiona. I didn't know you had such interest in court politics."

She smiled and shook her head. "None, really. I just—I am intrigued by the fate of this one woman. I wonder what it would have been like to be her. I wonder what it would be like to know her. She cannot have very many friends."

He laughed. "Then perhaps it is time for *you* to travel to Wodenderry and see if she needs her own Safe-Keeper! She must have many secrets she would like to share with someone she can trust."

She toasted him with her teacup. "Ah, now there is a good thought," she joked. "I am sure the princess and I would have much in common."

They talked for the next hour or so about the other sights Reed had seen in the royal city. He had taken a job with one of Robert's merchant friends and rented a room over a bookstore in a quiet part of town. In his little free time, he had explored many of the city's streets and alleys. Fiona listened with interest to his descriptions of paupers and lords, shopkeepers and traders, houses and mansions, and taverns and cathedrals.

"You'll have to go someday," he finished up. "It is so much more exhilarating than you can possibly imagine."

"Someday," she said, with such uncertainty that neither of them believed it. "For now, I am happy here."

Isadora arrived a week later, signaling, in Fiona's mind, the true start of the Wintermoon holiday. Time for Allison to move down to her grandmother's, time for the other beds to be aired out, time to replenish the stores of flour and eggs and butter so that all the traditional baking could begin.

But Fiona put only part of her attention to these tasks; with the rest of her energy, she was fretting about Isadora. "You look so thin!" she exclaimed when she first shepherded the Dream-Maker into the kitchen to warm up with a pot of tea. "Haven't you been eating?"

"Oh, I eat, but nothing tastes very good to me," Isadora said with a little shrug. "I'll grow fat again on your fine cooking, don't you worry."

"Are you sleeping? I can give you a serum that will stop you from waking up in the middle of the night."

"Now, that I'd be happy to take because—well—sometimes there is so much on my mind that I cannot fall asleep, to be honest," Isadora said. "I find—I wish—well, now. I'm an old lady."

Fiona set a piece of cake in front of her and sat next to her. "You wish what? We are alone. You can tell me any secrets." And she smiled, for she did not expect Isadora to comply.

But the Dream-Maker looked around the room, as if checking for eavesdroppers in the shadows, and she lowered her voice. "My dear, I am so tired of it," she said at last. "I do not wish to carry this burden anymore. It is time to hand it off to someone younger and stronger."

Fiona was silent a moment. "And is there a way you can do that, a way you can let go?"

Isadora shook her head. "I don't know. And I'm—I'm afraid to. What if the power passes to my daughter, who has had so much misery in her life already? How could I do such a thing to her? Even now she is expecting another child—and you know that they have all been stillbirths, every one. I should be at her side, but she does not want me there—I drag woe in my wake, she says. How can I say, 'Take this power from me,' and foist it on her instead? Doesn't she deserve some joy in her life?"

Fiona put her hand over Isadora's curled fist. "Let it go," she said in a quiet voice. "Release it. It is somebody else's time."

"I would, I would. Even knowing what might befall my daughter, I would," Isadora said, her fingers turning to entwine with Fiona's. "But there is so much left undone. So many dreams left unfulfilled. What if the burden passes from me, and *doesn't* go to my daughter? Suppose no one else picks it up at all? What if there are no more instances of magical joy in the world, all because I am too weak to inspire them?"

"Then the world will go on well enough. It is not your job to make everyone in it happy."

Isadora sighed. "No, but I would make you happy. And Reed. And Angeline. And Thomas. I would wave my hands and—like that!—each of you would be struck with a blinding joy. I would give each of you the dearest wishes of your heart, and then I would lie down and let this strangeness pass from my bones."

"We are all happy enough," Fiona said firmly. "You need not hang on even one more day just for us."

"Well—well—we'll see," Isadora said. She sounded so

tired that Fiona was seriously alarmed. "I may feel strong enough once the holiday is past. We shall see what happens after Wintermoon."

Fiona and Reed were out gathering the wreathing branches, so they didn't see the fine coach pull up at the house and discharge its passengers. Nonetheless, Fiona was not entirely surprised, returning with her bundles in her arms, to find three more guests on hand for Wintermoon—Angeline and Thomas, who were expected, and Robert Bayliss, who was not.

"I didn't think you'd mind," Angeline said to Fiona in an undervoice as Reed went over to greet the older man warmly. "With Victoria having died just two weeks ago, he is at such a loss. I didn't think anyone should have to be alone at Wintermoon."

"No, I'm happy to have him here," Fiona said. "I'll give him the sofa and move Thomas upstairs and make Reed sleep on the floor in his room. We shall have quite the houseful."

"Jillian went to Kate's for Wintermoon," Angeline added. "I made sure to find out, because I knew you would ask."

Fiona smiled. "My very next question."

Despite the fact that all of them respected Robert's grief—and, indeed, their old friend seemed to be wearing a perpetual look of numb loss—they managed to have a very pleasant evening meal. Reed had bought a half-cask of wine in town, and they toasted each other and told amusing stories of their adventures in the weeks that they had been apart. Isadora related the tale of the princess's visit and then some of the other unusual requests she had heard from her noble visitors.

"One woman—not so old, I thought, perhaps forty-five—she came to me as heavily veiled as the princess. And I was thinking, 'Don't bother to disguise yourself to me, for I don't know one of you court ladies from the other and I would forget your face in five minutes if you showed it to me now.' She came to me and told me her whole life was bitter and sad, and that she wanted the chance to make it worthwhile. Do something heroic. Well, I ask you, what could I possibly have said to that? How could I snap my fingers and confer on her the ability to be meaningful? I suggested she involve herself with some of the city charities, for there are all sorts of societies to aid orphans and other unfortunates, but she said that would not be good enough to atone. Atone for what, I wonder? I was as kind to her as ever I could be, but I wouldn't have known what to do for her even if I'd had the power."

Thomas was staring meditatively into his wine, apparently lost in some thought unconnected to Isadora's story. "I've always thought," he said at last, "that the most dangerous place for a Truth-Teller to live would be in Wodenderry. I've only been there a few times myself, and I didn't stay. But I keep thinking of what you said about the princess." He looked up, a sardonic smile on his face. "Now that I'm getting older, I begin to think about the things I'd like to do with my life before it ends. And one thing I'd like to do is tell a truth to the king. I don't know what that truth might be, but just think of it! To stand before royalty and tell him something no one else dared to say. I think that would be a rare privilege—though it might lose me my head."

Angeline pointed at him across the table. "You remind me," she said gaily. "Robert told me of a tradition he and his family used to observe at Wintermoon. They would stand in a circle around the bonfire, and each would whisper to the person on his left the dearest wish of his heart. And no one would repeat those wishes to anyone else—they all became Safe-Keepers for the year—but just the act of saying those wishes aloud would make them more likely to come true."

Robert smiled with an effort. "Well, we were children, and our dreams were very primitive," he said. " 'I want a new pair of boots for Wintermoon.' That was the sort of wish that very often came true."

"I'll cut snippets of truelove for each of us," Fiona said, "and we can throw them on the fire as we whisper our wishes."

"And we'll all gather again next year and report to each other if our wishes have been granted," said Angeline.

Fiona glanced around the table, augmented by one to, in some small way, make up for the loss of one. "Yes," she said, "all of us."

They spent the two days before Wintermoon braiding the wreaths and ropes of branches, baking sweet treats, and visiting with the neighbors. More snow fell, though the temperature was not so miserably cold as it sometimes was during the holiday season. Thomas and Reed and Robert spent the whole day of Wintermoon carefully laying the wood to construct the grandest bonfire Fiona had ever seen. After dinner, they lit the blaze and stood before it, admiring its reach and hunger. Its heat was so intense it drove them all a few paces away, to stand with their feet in the untrampled margin of snow.

Fiona passed out leaves of truelove and they arranged themselves around the fire. She wondered how deliberately some of them had taken their stances, though they appeared so casually to choose the confidant who would stand on their left. Fiona herself did not care which of this group heard the deepest wishes of her heart, though she was glad enough to have Angeline on her left and Reed on her right.

"I will begin," she said, and leaned over to whisper her own impossible desires in Angeline's ear. *"I wish I could meet my father and look again on my mother's face."* Angeline kissed her on the cheek, and Fiona tossed her truelove into the fire. It instantly flared to yellow flame and burned away.

Naturally, Fiona could not hear what Angeline murmured to Isadora, but she had a guess; she had, for a long time, suspected what Angeline might wish for were she to open her heart. Again, she did not wonder what Isadora whispered to Robert, for she was pretty sure how the words would go: *I want to lay this burden down.* Robert, she thought, said to Thomas: *It is not too late. Perhaps I can still sire a son.* Thomas probably repeated to Reed the observation he had made over dinner: *I would like to tell a single truth to the king.*

She was smiling as she leaned toward Reed, who stooped down to put his lips against her ear. He would tell her that he wanted to travel to Merendon or Marring Cross or Cranfield, someplace far away and exotic. He was the sort of man whose wish altered every year.

He said in a voice that only she could hear: *"I wish you were not my sister."*

She pulled back and stared up at him. He smiled, his face just faintly touched with sadness, and tossed his true-love into the fire.

Chapter Fifteen

They stayed up till dawn and slept past noon, and then they all ate meat pies and cakes and pastries till they were sick. Elminstra and half a dozen of her relatives arrived as they were finishing up the meal, and they exchanged small remembrances and many fond wishes.

"We're walking down to the village to see Lacey and all the others," Elminstra said. "Would any of you like to come with us?"

"Oh, I haven't seen Lacey in ages," Angeline said, getting to her feet. "Wait till I put my cloak on."

The rest of them declared themselves too lazy. "And I have to clean up the kitchen," said Fiona. "I'm going to set Robert and Reed to sweeping up the remains of the bonfire, though they don't know it yet."

Robert affected to be offended. "What? You put your guests to work? Angeline didn't mention that to me when she invited me to come for the holiday."

"But once we're done, I'll take you hiking," Reed promised. "I'll show you the creek! It's too cold to wade, of course, but we might catch something for dinner."

Once the others left and Isadora retired to her bed to sleep away the afternoon, Thomas and Fiona were left to clean the kitchen. "No, you chop some more wood for the stove," she told him, once she'd stumbled across his feet for the third time. "And then I'll make you some tea and you can just sit there quietly out of my way."

He grinned and complied, and she joined him at the table once the last dish was put away. "So how long will you be staying?" she asked, sipping from her own cup.

He shrugged. "It depends on Robert and Angeline, since I rode in with them. It must be nice to be a rich man, because that was the most comfortable coach I have ever been in."

Fiona smiled. "I like to have him here, and I know Reed enjoys his company. I cannot bring myself to be sorry that his wife is dead, though I know that is unkind of me."

He grinned. "Angeline seemed genuinely attached to her," he said, "but I find myself wondering if Victoria's death will do Angeline some good. It is not a truth I know, merely a suspicion I have."

Fiona tilted her head to one side. "Now, what do you mean by that?"

He countered with a question of his own. "Why do you think your aunt never married?"

"I always thought it was because the man she loved was already taken."

"Exactly. And now he's free."

Fiona laughed. "Oh, not Robert. He's much too neat and

fussy for Angeline. She speaks of him with great fondness, but she's more likely to matchmake for him, find him a pretty young girl from the village."

Thomas shrugged and sifted more sugar into his tea. "Perhaps we're wrong, then," he said. "Maybe she just never wanted to marry. Your mother never wanted to."

"She had you," Fiona said.

"She had me," he confirmed.

"Which perhaps is why Angeline never married."

Thomas just looked at her for the longest time, the expression on his face absolutely inscrutable. Then slowly, a faint wash of color reddened his cheeks, produced by some wild and random generation of new ideas. "I thought," he said, in a voice he tried to keep casual, "you were in the business of keeping other people's secrets."

Fiona smiled. "This was no confession whispered to me under the kirrenberry tree. This is merely something I have pieced together on my own."

"So it is not something you know positively."

She could not help it; she loosed a peal of laughter. "Oh, it never ceases to amaze me," she said, "what truths the Truth-Teller does not know."

"I am not the kind of man," he said, "that women pine away for."

"Indeed, no," Fiona said, still suffused with merriment. "So if I were you, I would be grabbing such chances at happiness as came my way."

He studied her a long time. "You wouldn't tell me this," he said, "if you didn't believe it to be true. And if you didn't believe it would benefit the one you loved most."

Fiona sobered a little. "There is nothing I would not do for Angeline," she said. "I believe her happiness is tied to you, and I believe her loyalty to my mother will not allow her to say so. I would guess she whispered your name to Isadora last night as we all stood around the fire. You were right about me, of course—there are some silences I have always thought it was better to break. But I will say nothing to her about this if you do not." She smiled a little. "It will be a secret between the two of us. You will see how silent I can be."

He was still watching her, his shadowed eyes narrowed and full of speculation. "And what secret was whispered to you last night?" he asked, in his old familiar quarrelsome way. "I think I would be less surprised to hear it than you were."

Now she was the one to flush, but she lifted her chin and looked defiant. "A secret I will keep for a while yet," she said.

He leaned forward. "Here's a truth for you," he said. "Time always goes by faster than you expect."

They did not have a chance to discuss it any longer—somewhat to Fiona's relief—because just then the front door flew open and Reed burst through, Robert at his heels.

"Fiona, Thomas—have you heard?" Reed exclaimed. "There is a royal procession arriving in the village!"

"A royal procession—you mean, the *king?*" she demanded.

"Yes, yes—at least, that is what everyone is saying!

There must be fifty riders and two coaches blazoned with the king's coat of arms—"

"How did you see this?" she asked. "I thought you were out by the creek."

He waved that aside. "We decided to go to town instead. I wanted Robert to meet Dirk at the tavern—but then we saw the coaches coming. Ned spotted them from two miles away with his new field glasses. I ran back to get you because I knew you would want to come see the king."

She came to her feet. "Indeed, yes! Let me get my boots on. But is he really coming *here?* Or is he just passing through town on his way somewhere else?"

Thomas had not moved, but now he looked up, straight at Fiona. "He is coming here," he said quietly, in that voice of certainty that meant some truth had been revealed to him and could not be doubted. "And he has come to look for . . . something that belongs to him."

Fiona put a hand to her heart, feeling faint for a moment, but neither Robert nor Reed appeared to catch the significance of that remark. "Here—your cloak—and you'll need some warm socks inside your boots," Reed said. "Hurry, Fiona! You don't want to miss him."

Thomas too was on his feet. "No," he said, heading to the main room and the box of muddy boots. "None of us wants to miss this."

They woke Isadora and insisted she come with them, though she said she had had enough of royalty during her weeks in Wodenderry. Nonetheless, to please them, she pulled on her boots and wrapped herself in her cloak and followed them out the door. Then, moving as fast as such an odd party could, the whole group headed directly toward the village, and they were not the only ones. In that mysterious way that news spreads over country towns, the word seemed to have gotten out to everyone that the king had come to Tambleham. The three or four houses they passed on the way stood empty; Fiona never doubted that all the residents were on their way to the town square. Their own group of five overtook several other parties, bigger and smaller, all of them heading for the main street of the village. "Did you hear?" they called to each other as they tramped through the mud and snow. "Did you hear? The king has come to town!"

They arrived to find the town thronged with people, everyone who lived within ten miles having somehow thought to gather here at this exact moment. The crowd was awestruck and well behaved, though, milling about at the fringes of the town square, no one willing to get too close to the cortege that had pulled up right by the village green. Reed had been right: The procession consisted of two carriages and what looked to be dozens of riders, both men and coaches decorated with the king's colors of scarlet and gold. Fiona had never seen horses so fine as those that pulled the elegant black carriages or those that carried the king's silent, watchful men.

Someone grabbed Fiona's arm and called her name. "There you are!" It was Angeline, and her face was bright with excitement. "I wanted to come back to get you, but I didn't want to leave! Are you all here? Reed and Isadora and everyone? The king has come to town—can you believe it?"

Fiona pushed forward through the mob, towing Angeline behind her. "Thomas, Reed, Robert—let's all get as close as we can. I want to see the king's face—I want to hear everything he has to say."

She met less resistance from the other villagers than she expected. Everyone else wanted to see the king, too, but everyone else was just a little afraid of being quite so close to royalty. Within a few minutes, she and her small group of friends had won their way to the very front of the crowd, till they were so close to the two carriages that they could see the brushstrokes on the coats of arms. The king's outriders drew a tight circle around the coaches, their spirited horses dancing a little from side to side. Fiona could get no closer, but she was near enough to see the door of one coach open, and a tall, severe figure step out and come to stand on a small dais in the center of the green.

The crowd was deathly quiet for a moment, and then everyone began to cheer. It was the king.

"His majesty, King Marcus!" one of the riders bawled out. "Her majesty, Princess Lirabel!"

For a second figure was stepping out of the second coach and coming to take her place beside the first. Fiona stood on tiptoe, as curious to see the woman as the man. The princess was nearly as tall as her father, dark like he was, her features as strict and grave. But, as Reed had said, her face looked kinder and sweeter, touched with sadness or disappointment. She stood behind and a little to one side of her father on the dais, her gaze fixed on his profile.

The king was staring down at the crowd, his eyes darting from face to face as if he was looking for someone he might recognize. "Who among you is mayor of this town?" he asked at last. His voice was thin and cold and carried easily to every listener in the throng.

The assembled people murmured amongst themselves and shrugged a little and did not answer. "Have you no mayor, no one who acts as leader?" the king repeated, his voice even colder.

Dirk the tavernkeeper shouldered his way forward. "I speak up now and then, sire, as the occasion demands," he called up to the stage. "I reckon I can speak for the village now."

A general undertone of approval meant the villagers were agreeable to making Dirk their spokesman. The king fixed his dark eyes on the barman. "Then I have a question to ask you," he said.

"Anything, sire."

"Eighteen years ago a baby was brought in secret to this village. It is news I have just this week learned from a young woman recently come to court."

Fiona's hand clenched on Isadora's arm. "Megan," she whispered. Isadora nodded but put her finger to her lips for silence.

The king was still speaking. "The child was a boy. No one knew his name or his parents' names. Yet he was brought in the arms of the Safe-Keeper from my court—who died by his own hand on his return from your village."

Now the crowd was full of muttering and speculation. Fiona caught more than a few people staring in the direction of her own little knot of friends. Dirk nodded calmly. "Aye, sire. That story is true."

The king's eyes seemed to glitter in the frosty air. "I would meet this boy," he said, his voice very stern. His daughter took a step back from him and trained her gaze on the wood of the stage. "I would meet this young man whom I believe to be my son."

Now the mutterings of the mob grew louder and more excited. Those in back were standing on tiptoe, looking around, trying to locate Reed in the crowd. Those nearest the king had already spotted Reed's tall form, and eager hands began to push all of them forward from behind. Fiona stumbled from the force of their enthusiasm; she saw Reed turn indignantly to upbraid someone behind him.

Dirk turned to survey the surging mass. "He's here, I believe, sire. I saw him earlier. Reed? There you are, lad! Come forward and meet your king."

Fiona felt someone's hand close iron-tight around her arm, but she didn't even look to see who grabbed her. She was watching Reed take an uncertain step toward the dais, then look back as if afraid to see what he was leaving behind, and then take another step. Dirk caught him by the shoulder and presented him to the king.

"This is Reed, sire, the child brought to the village in secret so long ago. He's a good boy—or rather, a fine young man. Any man would be proud to call him son."

Princess Lirabel seemed to grow smaller and thinner as

King Marcus bent down very low to look searchingly into Reed's face. "Are you that baby?" the king demanded. "There is nothing I would not do for a male child of my body, be he legitimate or bastard. Are you my son?"

"I don't know," Reed said.

Another voice rang above all the other murmurings of the mob. "He is not!" the speaker proclaimed in a voice meant for carrying news as far as it needed to go. "You have no son!"

And Fiona felt herself jerked forward by the man who was speaking, the man who had such tight hold on her arm. Thomas, whose greatest wish was coming true as he announced an unwelcome truth to the king.

The king, in fact, was glaring at Thomas with a most unnerving fury. He was still bent from the waist, the better to stare at the people arrayed before him. "Who are you?" King Marcus demanded. "What do you know about this boy and his parentage?"

"I am a Truth-Teller, and I have never told a lie," Thomas said calmly. He had dragged Fiona so close to the dais that they were merely inches from the king. Reed put his arm around Fiona, but she could not tell which of them was trembling. She looked up at the king, at his handsome, unhappy face, and watched his gaze flick between Thomas and Reed.

"You are telling me this child was brought here from the royal city eighteen years ago, in great secrecy, and yet he is not my son?" the king demanded, his voice very tight.

"He was not brought here that night. He was born here

to the Safe-Keeper herself. The child brought here that night was a girl."

And Fiona felt herself pushed forward one more time, till she was almost nose-to-nose with the king.

And then it was her wish came true.

"Look on your father's face, Fiona," Thomas said. "For you are the child brought here from Wodenderry that night."

The king straightened to his full height, disappointment and displeasure making his face look even bleaker. "Is this true?" he said at last, though it was unclear whom he asked.

Fiona found her voice. "True, sire," she said in a breath-less voice. "My mother—the Safe-Keeper who raised me—told me the story a few days before she died. My aunt can confirm it, for she was there the night I arrived. They did not know how valuable I was or why I might have been hur-ried from the city, so they thought to protect me by pre-tending I was the Safe-Keeper's daughter instead."

"Then—then—who is this boy?" the king demanded, pointing at Reed. Who stood stock-still beside Fiona, as dazed as the king, as astonished as everyone else in the now-silent crowd.

Thomas answered that. "The Safe-Keeper's son."

"Who is his father?" the king snapped, still clearly unwilling to believe the story that was unfolding around him. "Since everyone apparently believed him to be me."

"His father was a merchant from a nearby town," Thomas said, gesturing with his left hand. Behind her, Fiona heard a choked cry. "A man with whom the Safe-Keeper had

had a brief liaison when he believed his own fiancée had perished in an accident."

And so it was that Robert Bayliss's wish came true.

"Then—" the king said, and looked around him blindly, as if surprised to find himself before an unruly audience of people, hearing things he did not wish to know. "Then this boy is not my child. He is not my bastard son."

"You have no son," Thomas said, speaking with a certain relish. "You have never sired a son. You never will. You have only Fiona and Princess Lirabel. You must name the princess the heir to your throne, for you will beget no other legitimate children."

And so it was that the princess's wish came true.

The king turned clumsily toward the woman next to him on the stage, who seemed to have grown stronger and more regal in bearing with every one of Thomas's words. "Lirabel," he said, and his proud voice was broken. "Lirabel, help me to my carriage. Ride with me back to the city."

"Gladly, Father," she said, and her voice was rich and compassionate. "Step carefully here—take your courtier's hand. There. I will join you in a moment."

And as soon as her father was seated, Princess Lirabel stepped back onto the dais and crossed to the very edge. No one had moved. Reed and Thomas and Fiona were standing exactly where they had stood for the preceding momentous ten minutes, and the entire crowd waited still, expectant and hopeful.

Lirabel came to her knees at the edge of the stage and reached her hand out to Fiona. Unthinking, Fiona put her own in that strong, sure grasp. "Come to me in Wodenderry," the princess said in a voice so low only Fiona could hear it. "I would like to get to know my sister."

Fiona nodded, still too numb to say very much. "I would be glad to," she whispered. "In a few days. When everything is settled here."

Lirabel squeezed her hand and let it drop. Quickly, she rose to her feet, disappeared inside her father's carriage, and shut the door. The outriders cleared a space in the crowd for the two coaches to turn, and the trumpeter announced that the king's carriage was on the move. In a few moments, the king and his entire procession had disappeared down the road.

~ *Chapter Sixteen* ~

aturally, after all that, there was little chance that Fiona would be able to simply walk away. Angeline guided the exhausted Isadora out of the crowd, but the others stood fast, Reed and Thomas and Robert banding together behind Fiona to give her support. One by one, the villagers gathered around her, wishing her well and touching her cheek and claiming they had always known she was something special. She was as gracious as shock and wonder would allow, and she endured their good wishes for as long as she could.

Then, "Let's go home," she said to the men, and they broke away as gently as they could. Still, scattered groups of villagers waved to her from streetcorners and doorways as they passed, and Fiona waved back.

"You should not be so overcome," Thomas observed, though he held her right arm and lent her his considerable strength as they finally walked home. "You have known this secret for two years."

"True," she said in a faint voice. "But I suppose I did not

expect it to become known in such a public fashion."

"Could this have been a better day?" Reed said jubilantly. "Good news for everyone! Except the king, perhaps, and he did not deserve better news. I could not be happier!"

Fiona looked at him sideways, for he held her left arm, and beside him on the roadway paced Robert Bayliss. The merchant kept his gaze on the ground before him and had said nothing since they left the city center.

"So you are pleased to learn who your mother is, and your father," she said. "You have for so long wanted to know."

"Pleased!" Reed repeated. "Overjoyed!"

Robert came to a sudden halt, and they all perforce stopped alongside him. There was no traffic before or behind them, so they all just stood in the roadway and waited for him to speak.

"I did not know—your mother never told me," he said, his voice rapid and miserable. "I would have—I would have stood father to you all these years, either one of you, and yet she made me think—she never said—"

Fiona shook loose of Reed's hold and put a hand on Robert's arm. "My mother chose always to do what suited her best and caused the least distress to anyone else," she said. "I never doubted that this was news that had been deliberately kept from you."

"But you mustn't think—Victoria was dead, or so I thought, I would never have looked at another woman while I was betrothed to be married—"

"Everyone knows that," Fiona said. "And my mother knew she could never mortify Victoria by letting you know you had fathered a child while she was missing. It is only now that the pieces could come together and the secret could be shared."

Reed stepped forward and put his hand on Robert's shoulder. "I have the father I would have chosen if I could have picked from the whole world," he said in a quiet voice. "I will be the best son you could have imagined, if you will let me."

There was that sound again, a choked cry, and then Robert was openly weeping. "You and I will continue walking," Fiona said to Thomas, "and let the two of them sort everything out."

Angeline met them at the door of the cottage with her fingers to her lips. "Isadora is sleeping," she whispered. "I think this day has been almost too much for her."

Fiona slipped by her into the welcome warmth. "I think this day has been almost too much for all of us," she said.

The three of them sat around the kitchen table, drinking mint tea and talking quietly. "I still don't understand," Fiona said. "Why it was so important to disguise me. What's another bastard daughter to the king, after all?"

"There had been two others, delivered to highborn ladies in the years between Lirabel's birth and yours," Thomas said. "Both of those little girls died in infancy."

Fiona felt her eyebrows rise. "From . . . illness?"

Angeline shook her head. "They had been murdered.

And the royal Safe-Keeper knew it, for the queen had confided her dark deeds to him. And he confided in me, the day he left you in my arms. He had done what he could to protect you—acting as *Safe*-Keeper indeed, though we who keep secrets are not always so active in defending them."

Fiona slanted a look at Thomas. "Some of us are," she said.

"I still don't understand," Thomas complained. "If someone had tracked that Safe-Keeper all the way to Damiana's house, wouldn't Reed have been in just as much danger as Fiona?"

"We thought about that," Angeline admitted. "But we thought we could still keep him safe. We could have brought in any Truth-Teller—even you!—to swear that he was not the king's bastard. We thought if Damiana claimed Fiona as her own, no one would think to ask questions about her."

"A little chancy still," Fiona said.

"All secrets are," Angeline replied.

"Did you know the other secret as well?" Thomas asked Angeline. "All these years, did you know who Reed's father was?"

Angeline shook her head. "I thought it was you. Though you and Damiana were not very close until the children were a little older. But I thought—well—that I had missed some earlier moment when you fell in love."

Now Thomas was the one to shake his head. "I would have claimed them—either one of them. That's a truth even a Safe-Keeper wouldn't have kept from me."

"All the secrets are out now," Angeline said. "All the truths told. All the wishes come true."

"Not quite all of them," Fiona said.

Thomas looked at her. "What's still left undone?" he asked.

But she merely smiled and shook her head. She was still a Safe-Keeper—for a while yet.

Robert and Reed came back late, having stayed for a few glasses of ale at Dirk's tavern, buying a few rounds for the other patrons and generally celebrating their newfound connection. Fiona wanted to talk to Reed, but not in his inebriated state, and so she sent both of them on their way to bed and retired to her own room. She couldn't sleep, of course. For the longest time, she just lay on her mattress, listened to Isadora's breathing, and stared at the shadows on the walls.

So much had already changed, but there were changes still to come.

In the morning, she rose as soon as she heard quiet footsteps descending the stairs. It was Reed, as she had known it would be, for he was always an early riser. She hastily dressed and went out to join him in the kitchen.

"It snowed last night," he said, speaking in a whisper to avoid waking Robert, who was sleeping on the sofa. "Do you want to go walk through the fresh snowdrifts?"

"Yes," she said, and they put on their boots and crept out.

"How's your head?" she asked once they'd stepped outside. The world was a frigid white scene of ice and gauze; their feet crunched through the crisp top layer of snow with every stride they took. The air felt freshly washed or newly made, cold and delicious when they breathed it in.

Reed laughed. "Fine, if you're talking about the ill effects of ale. In a whirl, if you're talking about the aftereffects of yesterday's audience with the king."

"Everything is different now," she agreed.

He surprised her with his response. "But everything is better."

She glanced up at him as they tramped along. His strong young face looked rested and serene; his smile was wider than ever. "You mean, you were happy to find out you were not the king's son?"

He shrugged. "I was happy to find out I was *someone's* son, and to find that I'm Robert's! I couldn't ask for a better father. And to know at last who my mother was—to have all the questions answered—it makes me feel like I belong in the world, after all this time of wondering."

"I told you before, you make your own belonging."

He peered down at her from his much greater height. "So does that mean you still belong here—in a small village—when you know you're the daughter of the king?"

She sighed. "I do foresee some upsets in my life."

They had come to an old wooden fence that separated their property from some open space. Reed brushed the snow off the top bar, then lifted Fiona up to sit. He leaned on his elbows beside her.

"This is what I expect to happen," he said quietly. "You will go to the royal city from time to time, and make friends with your sister, and learn how to behave in the presence of your father. You will return to Tambleham now and then, but it will never be your permanent home the way it has been for so long. There will be other pressures at work on you, other hands reaching for you. After all this time, it is you who will be the restless one, and I the one who stays in one place."

"But if I leave, who will be Safe-Keeper in Tambleham?" she asked. "Who will live in our mother's cottage?"

He turned and leaned his back against the railing. "Allison and Ed will live in our mother's house, I imagine, since she understands the garden so well. I will live in the house being built on Angeline's land."

"You!" she exclaimed. "But I thought—won't you be going to Lowford to live with Robert?"

He nodded. "I'll go for a while. But I won't stay. I belong in Tambleham, and I have work to do here."

She looked down at him. "*You're* going to be Safe-Keeper of the village."

He nodded. "Isn't it funny? I knew that people were always telling me secrets. I knew how to keep them. But I thought it was because—because I had been raised in the house with a Safe-Keeper and her daughter. But it was because a Safe-Keeper was my mother, and I inherited her ability to keep silence." He glanced at her. "I don't know how you managed to learn such a difficult thing all on your own."

She smiled. "I was never as good at it as I wanted to be.

212

Thomas was right about me. I'm more interested in truth than secrets."

"And we've had our share of both this past day," he said.

"Secrets revealed, truths proclaimed, and everyone's dreams come true," she said.

He kept his eyes on the white vista before him. "Only one of mine," he said quietly. "The chance to know my father. I told you another wish the other day."

She smiled a little. "We will work on that wish when you come home from Lowford," she said. "I still have one of my own to fulfill, and it's haunted me for longer."

He tilted his head up at her, squinting a little in the sun. "You want to find your mother," he said.

She nodded. "If she's still alive. You make your own belonging—but you have so few chances at love. Seeing Robert's face when he looks at you makes me want to see her face when she looks at me."

"But you'll come back to me?"

She put her hand on his shoulder. "As you've always come back to me."

Two days later, Robert's carriage arrived at the door, and Robert, Reed, Angeline, and Thomas all piled in. "I'll be gone a month, I expect," Reed told Fiona as he hugged her good-bye. "When will you go to the royal city?"

"I don't know yet," she said. "I might not be here when you get back. But soon."

"Soon," he said, and kissed her cheek, and climbed in beside his father.

Angeline hugged her next. "I am almost afraid to go," her aunt said. "So much has happened in a few short days! What else will happen as soon as I turn my back?"

Fiona laughed. "Oh, no! I've had my share of adventures. It's somebody else's turn to engage in surprises."

"I'm not sure yours are all done yet," Thomas said.

Fiona hugged him as well. "And your life?" she asked innocently. "It does not have a twist or two still in it?"

Angeline smiled. "Oh, Thomas's life is always full of excitement. He travels from town to town, spreading good news and bad, and he is often just one step ahead of an angry villager."

He shook his head. "No longer. I'm going to settle down and let people come to me with their questions and their disputes."

Angeline looked at him quickly. "Settle down! But where?"

He took her elbow and helped her into the carriage. "In Lowford. On a street or in a house or in a room as near to you as I can get."

Angeline froze with one foot on the pulldown steps. "Thomas! What do you—what are you saying?"

He laughed and urged her forward. "You'll have to invite me in once we arrive in Lowford, and I can explain in more detail."

And so it was that Angeline's wish came true.

Fiona was smiling as she stood by the gate and waved, sad to see almost all of her best-loved friends and relatives driving away, but fixing part of her mind on all the chores that were still left to do. There was still her own last wish to be granted, and another one that she knew of—

And another one that she'd heard rumors of, but it was somebody else's dream, and she didn't know if it might really come true.

Chapter Seventeen

sadora stayed two more days, "too tired," she told Fiona, "to even *think* about flagging down some chance traveler and asking to be taken to whatever remote, dream-forsaken village he happens to be traveling to next. Besides, I keep waiting—" She stopped.

"Waiting for what?" Fiona asked.

"Waiting for word from my daughter. She knows I come here for Wintermoon, and surely she will tell me—or not, if the news is so bad that she cannot bear to write it—"

"You just rest while you can," Fiona commanded. "When you feel strong enough, I'll write your daughter for you, and good or ill, we'll find out the story."

So Isadora dozed away the next two days while Fiona made preparations for travel. She visited with Elminstra to exclaim over the events of the last few days and to discuss with Allison the idea of renting Damiana's cottage to the newlyweds. Soon, everything was ready; there were only a few more pieces to put in place. Fiona knew that, like

Isadora, she was waiting, simply waiting, but she didn't know what else to do.

Late in that second afternoon, she returned to her own house to find her guest weeping on the sofa. "Isadora! What's wrong? Did you hear from your daughter?" Fiona exclaimed, running across the room and flinging her arms around the Dream-Maker. "I'm so sorry—"

But Isadora, when she turned to face Fiona, was smiling through her tears. "She had—she bore—it's a baby boy, and he's healthy! She wants me to come see him, come as soon as I can. She's not—the curse will not pass to her; she is safe from this misery. I am so happy that I cannot stop crying."

Fiona laughed, and then she cried too, and she read the letter, and she joined Isadora in speculating on who among the Tambleham townspeople might be persuaded to head for Thrush Hollow in the next few days. Not till they were eating dinner a few hours later did Isadora tilt her head and seem to listen to a soundless interior voice. She put her fork down and stared at Fiona across the table.

"Fiona. It's gone," she said, her voice a mix of regret and wonder.

"What's gone?"

"The power. I don't feel it anymore," Isadora said simply. "It's not just that my daughter will not inherit the ability to make dreams come true—I don't have the talent anymore either."

"Then where did it go? Or did it? Is the world without a Dream-Maker now?" Fiona asked.

Isadora shook her head. "I don't know. I don't know. I hope not, though. What a sad place this would be if we could never put our trust in dreams. But, oh, I am so happy that the power has passed away from me!"

And so it was that Isadora's wish came true.

Isadora left with Ned the blacksmith on the following day, neither Isadora nor Fiona bothering to mention that, with her powers gone, Isadora would not be able to grant him any special wishes in return for this favor. But Ned was a kind enough man; Fiona was sure he would have taken Isadora as a passenger anyway, though he might have charged her for the privilege. Fiona smiled as she waved good-bye and blew kisses to the happy old woman on her way to meet her grandson.

She passed the day quietly, cleaning up behind all her recent guests and checking to see how low her stores of food were. She wrote a letter to Reed, and one to Angeline, and thought about writing her half-sister but decided she would rather wait till they were better acquainted. Early winter dark came, and she put on the tea to boil, then later she made a very good dinner out of bread and cheese and leftover pie.

It was fairly late when she heard the sound of a solitary horse approaching her gate and coming to a halt. She lifted her head when the hoofbeats slowed and did not pass by, and she was at the door just as the knocker sounded. She opened the door to find a heavily veiled woman standing on the front stairs.

"Is this the house of the Safe-Keeper of Tambleham?" the visitor asked in an attractive voice that had the soft accent of the southern gentlewoman.

"Indeed it is. Do you have a secret you wish to confide?" Fiona said. "Please come in out of the cold."

The lady stepped inside and appeared to be looking around through her veil, assessing the hominess of the furnishings and the comfortable warmth of the room. "A secret, perhaps—a question, perhaps—there are many things I have to say," the woman said. "If you have a few moments to spare me."

"As many moments as you like. Take off your coat. I will put more water on to boil."

Soon enough, they were both sitting at the kitchen table sipping tea. The visitor still felt the need for secrecy; she did not remove her veil, but lifted the bottom edge so she could take a dainty drink. Through the tight black mesh, Fiona could catch a hint of fine, fair hair and eyes that appeared to be a faded blue. It was very difficult to tell much else, though Fiona thought the woman might be about Angeline's age—somewhere in her mid-forties. Not old, but starting to feel the accumulation of years.

Just now, the woman was glancing around the kitchen as if looking for someone who was missing. "I was told," she said, blowing on her tea through her veil, "that the Dream-Maker of this kingdom often stays at this house."

"She does. She left just this morning. Did you have something you wanted to ask her?"

The woman took a sip from her cup. "Or something to tell her. I—I saw her when she was in Wodenderry a few weeks ago. I came to her to ask her about a dream. And I think—I'm not sure—but I feel so strange—"

"Ah," Fiona breathed. "That was you."

Though it was impossible to read the woman's expression through her veil, her confusion was evident in her voice. "What was me? What do you know? I went to the Dream-Maker to ask—to say—to beg her to give my life some meaning. My whole life has been nothing but tragedies and mistakes. Hurts I have dealt to other people, wounds that have been inflicted on me. I wanted—I asked her—is there not some way to reverse all that? To confer on my life some grace and beauty?"

"And do you think you have found that way?" Fiona asked.

"I don't know. It's very strange. I woke up yesterday and felt so odd, as if my toes and fingers were tingling, but I wasn't cold, and I wasn't sick, and the sensation has since gone away. But I feel altered somehow. And then my maid came to me, overjoyed. Her mother, who had been so sick, sat up in bed and was well. And the man who lives in the house next door—a man who needs money for so many reasons I cannot begin to list them all—he came laughing to my gate. His uncle had just left him an inheritance. It seemed everywhere I turned that day, good fortune had befallen someone I knew. Someone I had spoken

220

to just the day before. And I thought—I wondered—but can it be? Can the power of the Dream-Maker have passed into me?"

Fiona put her hands to her cheeks, for this was the dream she had hoped for, the one dream besides her own that she most wanted to see come true. "I think it has," she said, her voice very rapid. "For when Isadora left this place, she knew the power had fled from her. But we did not know if it had settled in anyone else's hands."

"Then I am—I am the Dream-Maker? I am—where I go—I will bring happiness to others? All this tragedy, all these woes—they did some good after all? For I know the Dream-Maker's life is not an easy one. I know it is only at the cost of my own happiness that I bring joy to others. But I have paid that cost, over and over again. I have given up so much."

"And what is the first thing you gave up?" Fiona asked in a low voice.

The woman looked around the room, and the despair in her voice made her words shake. "My child, my daughter, for her own safety, I sent her away so many years ago. I thought—I had heard—this might be the very cottage where she was given refuge." The woman turned her face toward Fiona's. "You might be the very girl," she whispered. "You look so much as I had imagined."

"I am that girl," Fiona said, stretching her hand out across the table to take hold of her mother's fingers. "I am your daughter. Tell me your name, and then tell me my story, and we will learn each other's dreams and secrets."

"I am Melinda," the woman said.

"I am Fiona. For so long I have wanted to look on my mother's face."

Melinda reached up to pull aside her veil. And then it was that the Dream-Maker made Fiona's last wish come true.

Turn the page for a taste of

The
Truth-Teller's
TALE

CHAPTER ONE

hat would you say if I told you there was a time a Safe-Keeper told a secret, a Truth-Teller told a lie, and a Dream-Maker did everything in her power to make sure a wish went astray? Believe what I tell you, for I am a Truth-Teller, and every word I say is true.

No sisters could ever have been less alike than my twin and I. To the casual observer, we looked exactly the same, for we both had wheat blonde hair and exceptionally pale skin, and the bones of our faces had an identical structure. But Adele was right-handed; she parted her hair on the right; her right eye was blue and her left eye was green. I was left-handed; I parted my hair on the left; my left eye was blue and my right eye was green. We each saw in the other the very same face, the very same figure, we saw in the mirror every morning.

You could not blame people for getting us mixed up—until they knew our personalities, and then it should have been easy to tell us apart. For Adele was devious and secretive. She would listen to whispered conversations between strangers and learn all manner of interesting revelations, but never repeat a word. From the time we were quite little, she could lie with utter sincerity, so that you never knew if she was making up a story or concealing a dreadful fact. I, on the other hand, tattled on everyone. If a boy pushed a girl into a puddle, I told his mother about it that very afternoon. If your bow was crooked, your shoes didn't match, or your hair was a mess, I would be sure to let you know. At school, when the teacher asked a question, I could hardly wait to be called on before I would blurt out the answer. Words wouldn't stay inside me, whereas Adele could go days without bothering to make conversation at all. If such a thing were possible, I would have said that I was as transparent as a window—that light and color and information passed through me as if I was not even there—whereas Adele was as opaque and mysterious as a dark curtain motionless before that window on a starless winter night.

She was, in many respects, the most irritating person I knew. If you were ready to leave the house and you called her, sometimes she would not answer. If you wanted her opinion about a dress you were wearing or a boy you liked, she would merely look at you and give you that enigmatic smile. She never told you if she had fallen down and hurt herself or if a girl in school had been mean to her or if she had found out what your parents had bought you as a Wintermoon gift. She could be difficult, obstructive, confusing, and maddening, all without saying a word.

I would not trade her for all the gold in Wodenderry.

2